# ANOTHER TIME

by

## Joseph Hullett

Answer Publications
San Juan Capistrano, California

Published by Answer Publications
27511 Vantage Circle
San Juan Capistrano, CA 92675, USA
www.answerpub.com

ISBN: 978-0-9844597-5-9

Produced in the United States

---

ACKNOWLEDGMENTS

The nidus of this work was my prize-winning short play *True Believer*, produced and directed by Jill Forbath for the West Coast Play Competition Festival. Adapted as a short story, it was included in my collection *Men With Women*. Other elements of the story-cycle first appeared in *War, Literature and the Arts, Palo Alto Review*, and *Mind in Motion*.

**For Cpl. Don Trupiano, USMC**

And other sad shadows who went searching for something lost an age and a world away. Semper Fi ... in my fashion.

# ANOTHER TIME

by

## Joseph Hullett

## Contents

Unnumbered: The Madman

Uncounted: Time Out of Mind

## UNNUMBERED: THE MADMAN

I'm pulling my third-straight, two-to-two shift, almost last call, like totally sleepworking, and this talking-ass monkey has my ears about to bleed.

"Give it a rest, old timer," I say finally. "I wasn't even born back then. What's it to me?"

"I'm not an old timer," he says, tapping his empty glass. "I'm an *other* timer."

I slosh in more Jack D, and draw what I need from his pile of change. It's strictly pay-to-pour for a dude who knocks 'em back a whole shift with nothing showing but shiny, freaking eyes.

"An *other* timer?" I say, shaking my head. "Try full-on demento, man."

He slugs down half the whiskey and wipes his chin with his wrist.

"Listen to me, kiddo. If you think a motor-mouth makes me crazy, you're cracked yourself. Words are the all-clear signal. Silence is the duck-and-cover. Take it from someone who's seen the elephant. I've known madmen. *Real* madmen. Known them face to face, like you and me across the bar here, and the craziest rarely made a peep. Take Jessup, for example. Jessup was certifiable. And quiet? Like snowfall.

"No, you'd never find Jessup blabbing like this. With me, it's because … well, actually, it's the job, see? When *I'm* pouring, I'm as tight-lipped as you are. But plop a bartender stool-side and suddenly he's a soliloquist.

"What? You don't believe it? That's because you're green, but wait and see. You're staring at an occupational hazard – a repetitive strain injury from years of listening dumbly like some plaster Jesus that doesn't hear a word, when, the thing is, *we do*.

"And we *remember* what we hear. All those stories become tangled inside with scraps of our own that we can't trashcan. Words, pictures, sounds." He thumps a fist into his chest. "Right here! Tangled scraps reeking with grief and guilt and love and rage and pity. Scraps smoldering like a pile of gasoline soaked rags. Ignore them long enough, kiddo, and all hell erupts. Just wait. You'll see. One day every smoldering scrap will still be right here in your chest. Hot! A heat inside. You'll feel it. Right here!"

He's pounding his chest like he's trying to hack up a fish bone. I see things are heading south, so I stomp the brake.

"Get loud, you get gone, *other* timer."

He raises his hands and skids to a whisper.

"It's cool, man. I'm cool. You think I'd make a scene? We're *colleagues*, right? And it's not like I'm drunk. I can't *get* drunk."

He downs the rest of his whiskey in a single salute.

"Hit me again, will you? Detroit was just a day trip. Home is an overnight bus ride and I don't sleep much without a little help."

I tap his change pile. He paws a twenty from his pocket and lays it across the silver. I fill his glass. One swallow and he's off again.

"Home for me is Ontonagon, a way-north town you'll never see. It's here in Michigan, but barely. Run your finger west across a map of the Upper

Peninsula and, if your eyes are good, you'll spot it
– a speck of no consequence on Lake Superior
just north of Wisconsin, a few klicks shy of the
Porcupine Mountains."

Talking to my back while I ring his drink, he
catches me rolling my eyes at the mirror,  but
does it stop him? Not even a speed bump.

"Cut loose from the Marines back in '72, I
washed up there and took root." He pauses a sec
and shakes his head. "No ... that's wrong. It
makes me sound like a coconut. Truth is, I
bought a ticket; I boarded a bus; I got off when it
stopped. Ontonagon was a choice, like everything
else is a choice, so you're probably wondering
why there?"

That *wasn't* what I was wondering.

"Well, first of all, I remembered the town from
a last fling camping trip I took before I enlisted,
but beyond that? How do I explain something
that's half loony? Something that has to be
foreign to you? How could you translate it?"

"Sounds hopeless," I say hopefully.

"No. No, it's not, because ... okay, here's what
I think. I think each of us has a kind of Rosetta
Stone. It's buried in us, that part, so we need to

dig it out, brush it off, restore it. But then we can match the hieroglyphics of what other people say and do against the things we think we know about ourselves – feelings we remember, meanings we suspect, all of it wrong, of course, but close enough, see!

"Say I said I was feeling lost back then; say I said I was backtracking like people do when they're lost, and that, remembering Ontonagon was like stumbling onto a signpost. Those are words, just words, *foreign* words for the good they'd do you to know what I really mean, the part inside. But look back and you'll find some near match of your own. You took a bad turn yourself once, right? Maybe it was dark. Maybe you were alone. Kicking yourself was no good, because you didn't know where you went wrong. But thinking back, you remembered a spot that stood out, and you said to yourself, I knew where I was back then, knew where I was going and even how to get there. Sound familiar?

"If it does, you'll recall how remembering that spot stirred something in you. A feeling like baptism, I bet, if that's something you know, or something else. But whatever it was for you, you felt what I felt remembering Ontonagon – you felt the washing, the lifting, the salvation, the certainty you'd find your way clear again if you could just get back to that remembered spot. And if you summon those feelings now, if you let yourself feel them again right now, you'll see the unseeble part of me through the lens of *you*. Distorted? Of course. Through a glass darkly? Yes! But close enough. Close enough, don't you see?

"Well, that was Ontonagon when I finally bailed from the VA Hospital after 'Nam. In my head it was good, and it was about the last good thing I remembered at the time.

"It's still a good thing, for that matter. Deep woods, deep water. Not many people, and people you can care about, even the bad ones. The baseball is bush league – that's a downer – but the fishing and hunting are good, or hiking and skiing if you've had your fill of killing. And unlike most little towns up that way, Ontonagon has a golden goose – a corrugated box mill that provides a year-round livelihood.

"Of course, people there, especially youngsters like you, they look around, they look back, and, don't you know, they feel lost, too. They imagine other places where it's all good, or it will be, and season done, they blow away. Population was down to 2800 last count. The evergreens, I guess. Old growth from another time.

"But I was telling you about the madman, wasn't I? Jessup, not me. Funny ... Jessup couldn't sleep either, not when the madness had him. Most madmen are that way. He was supposed to take pills, and sometimes he would, sometimes he wouldn't. He had no wife or kids, no father or mother that I knew of, but, lucky enough, he had a brother who policed his pills and fetched him out of trouble. Brothers like that are rare, I bet, but then, family is strange and you never know.

"Anyway, when Jessup swallowed the pills his brother fed him, I often saw him shuffling down Lake Street, empty-handed and aimless. Those times, he passed without a nod which was strange since, other times, when he refused the pills, he found his way to the Harbor – that's my place, the Harbor Bar – and for hours on end sat scribbling silently on yellowed pieces of paper. The papers were his so-called manuscript – more accurately a bundle of loose scraps crushed between stained shirt boards cinched together with green rubber bands. The guy was harmless enough, so I let him sit, but listen to me. The scribbling was the thing!

"According to his brother, he began the scribbling when the madness first seized him, not long after they retired him from the box mill. The brother would always know when the madness was stirring again, because suddenly Jessup returned to his frenzied scribbles. It was a sign. Like bleeding palms or a bleeding heart. The manuscript so marked those purgatory periods of mute starvation and tortured insomnia that the brother often considered burning it, as if the flames might cauterize Jessup's wounds. But something in his brother's fevered attention to the wretched thing always swayed him. So when Jessup finally abandoned the manuscript – as inevitably he did – the brother saved it in a cedar chest where Jessup went looking when the bleeding broke once more.

"Sometimes I wonder why the brother did that, why he saved it, but I forever find "whys" to spare. He was frightened. He was bored. He was

angry. Maybe he did it out of love. Maybe out of meanness. Maybe the brother was crazy, too. I mean, crazy runs in families, right?

"Old-timers at the bar remembered Jessup from his mill days as a good-natured regular. Something in the madness must've urged his return. Maybe some memory of a feeling from before the madness. Whatever it was, it drew him back to the Harbor to sit scribbling with a stub pencil over his precious bits of paper.

"I was curious. I wanted him to say something, but he was mute, consumed in the motion of his pencil. I wondered if, perhaps, the motion itself said something – like waving semaphores – so I listened with my watching. And since ghost souls gravitate toward being heard as surely as they home in on light, eventually I gained a glimpse at his scribbles.

"Hesitantly, like a mother surrendering her child to a stranger, the madman extended his papers. In a rusty voice of leaky-steam whispers, he proclaimed that he had mathematically proven the existence of God!

"I felt cheated. God was a futile sum whose bottom line I knew. Still ... I thought I might find *something* in the papers, perhaps some unintended pearl his obsession had formed. I rifled through handbills, napkins, matchbook covers, his birth certificate, old pay stubs from the mill, calendar pages, death notices from the Gazette – each and every scrap dense with penciled figures.

$$[(0x0)/0] \; x \; \{0 + (0 - (0+0)/0 - 0/0 \; x$$
$$(0/(0x0)0/0\} + 00 \; x \; [(0\text{-}0) \; x \; 0 - 00 \; ...$$

On and on. Zeroes. A mad cortege of zeroes. Of *nothing*.

"But his eyes! They burned with a plea that I see the scribbles as he did. That I see beyond the ashen shadows on the paper to the fire that blazed in the dungeon where his chained soul howled. A man knows when he's understood. He sees the other's eyes ignite like a candle touched by a match. I looked away, hiding my eyes, and could only shake my head in a silence that was to him, I imagine, the silence of a bell ringing impotently in the vacuum of a bell jar.

"Perhaps his savage god did exist, because he returned to his scribbles and never again offered them.

"But listen, here's my point. While I'll never know what he *meant*, I think I know how he *felt*. I mean ... okay, like I said before, you never *really* know that, but ... as strange, as alien as he was, it was *as if* I knew, because I've felt something *like* he felt. In my own way, sure, but, listen to me ... that limping simile is close enough!

"It's that fire inside. That rage to wail *'I shall tell you all! I shall tell you all!'* And I – I *am* calm! It's a line from a poem. A poem, that's all. I read a little. Just listen to me. Listen!"

He's waving his arms, sounding def ready to blow, so I grab his shoulder. He jerks back so hard, he almost munches it off the stool.

"You don't have to put your hands on me, okay? Just forget it. I'll sit quiet as a corpse. I learned that lesson forty years ago at the Veteran's Hospital right here in Detroit. Sit quietly and they keep their hands to themselves."

He slams a lid on it. Dementos can do that, but not for long. The guy is like a pressure cooker and, sure enough, the words soon start to sputter out.

"That's why I rode a bus all day," he says. "Not the lesson, the hospital. Just yesterday I heard they took a wrecking ball to that old charnel house, and, long ride or not, I had to come see. Don't ask me why, though. I tried counting 'whys' on the trip down, but kept losing track. My favorite was that I needed to see what the world looked like without that place in it.

"But the Goddamm thing is still here, isn't it? Closed, but waiting, mothballed for another time. For guys coming home from the crusades, or if that's too soon, the time after. There's always another time.

"I scoped out the place anyway. The cabbie called me crazy and ditched me to hump it back, which was fine, because it gave me some private time with that old donjon – two hold-outs in a last-one-standing contest.

"Crunching through dead leaves, I scouted the perimeter fence. It was a good fence, too! Sturdy and higher than I could climb. A ring of barren elms and oaks just inside the fence circled the grounds like sentries, but all ten were just out of reach.

"Funny ... being back there resurrected things long dead. As a kid I had buried this little counting demon I had for a while – no big deal until 'Nam dug it up and transformed it into a monster. The VA Docs called it a compulsion. I also brought home an obsession with even numbers, especially the number ten, which was a soul shaker. I thought I had put those Goddamm zombies down for good, but back in the shadow of that hospital, it was like old times, me counting and recounting those ten trees, trying to make them come out nine or eleven. I'm grateful the leaves didn't spook me, or I'd still be out there counting."

The old guy eyeballs me and snorts, "C'mon, kiddo, lighten up. It's a *joke* already! You never get the leaves right. Always a breeze. Only a madman counts *leaves*."

He's nodding silently as if he's remembering something.

"You know, it's strange ... picturing it again right now, I see those trees still had color. Holdout leaves dotted the branches with a thin, exhausted ocher hue, that rusty color trees turn when the leaves won't let go. And it surprises me, because the day I said good-riddance – a dead-winter, ground-dusted-white-with-frost day – everything was black-and-white, and black-and-white is how I've remembered the place for forty years. Black and white and cold.

"It still seemed cold to me, although it's not really cold yet, is it? Regardless, the air *smelled* cold, so I must have smelled the coming cold. Don't scoff. It's real enough, that smell. Haven't you ever seen a squirrel rooting through fallen leaves and suddenly he rears up and sniffs? Watch him next time, how he goes back to his business with a whole different rhythm, because he smells the cold coming and everything, *everything* is changed.

"Listen, who knows? I was yanking hard on the chain and maybe all I smelled was that iron gate against my face. But the thing is, trees or not, the building *itself* rose exactly as I remembered it, like something *bad* in a bad dream. I felt swallowed in it's cold, black shadow, and I know you're thinking the sky was gray today and nothing *had* a shadow, and you're right! Nothing did. Except *that* place. Crazy, but true, I tell you. I felt it. A cold shadow as real as the rocks in my hand. As real as the sound of breaking windows ..."

The old guy's voice peters out, and he's staring at nothing with those shiny eyes. Not a good sign at last call.

"Ground Control to Major Tom," I say, careful not to touch him this time. "Your circuit's dead."

He shakes his head as if he'd walked into a spider web. "... What?! What'd you say? I was, uh ... *listening* to something."

"Last call," I say.

"Goddamm!" he mutters, glancing at his watch. "Better hit it hard then. Ontonagon is a long ride and I won't sleep without a little help."

"So you told me," I say.

The glint in his eyes goes nova. "Occupational hazard, kiddo."

"What's that? Repeating myself?"

He grins like some ass-hat winning a lame bar-bet.

"No," he says. "*Remembering.*"

## 1. SING GODDAMM

"Ontonagon. Last stop. Ontonagon. Everybody off!"

The baldy bus driver had grunted maybe a couple dozen words since Mackinaw – most of them "Pipe down!" Suddenly he's barking at empty seats just to hear his own Goddamm noise. Probably an old Marine drill instructor who forgot to take the swagger stick out of his ass.

"Aye-aye, sir!" I snapped.

His face puckered as if from a bad belch. Definitely not Corps, just some pogue.

Scrambling behind him, I lit from the Greyhound hatchway directly into a Lake Superior blizzard. The wind rocked me like rotor wash, sparking a flashback that almost sent me diving for cover. The driver clawed open the luggage hatch, tossed my seabag into the sidewalk snow, and scurried into the depot.

I was tempted to follow, but I needed to finish my business and scrounge a bunk for the night. That was about as far ahead as I was thinking just then. Come morning, if I hadn't frozen, I'd choose my next move. Blowing on my hands, I shouldered the seabag and humped toward the water. Wind-driven snow peppered my face like birdshot. Goddamm, it was cold!

That's the trouble with places remembered from another time. I remembered *summer* in the Upper Peninsula, a few good weeks in '70, two years back – a last-fling trek I took with my blood-brother, Don, prior to boot camp. But this was winter, or more accurately some uncalendared season beyond winter. Saginaw, where I grew up, had winter: a touch of snow, a taste of zero. This was the season of hell freezing over. The howling wind was Satan, trapped in the solid Lake, cursing God.

Visibility was zip. Ghostly streetlamps hovered in a cloud of blown snow. A rust-pocked pickup, groaning and slip-sliding, materialized from the cloud. The mittened driver, surprised to find a fellow madman out in the storm, shot me a cheery thumbs-up. Saluting as the truck crunched past, I watched it disappear again like an apparition.

Funny how a simple gesture like two strangers raising empty hands can sometimes set you to laughing and weeping at the same time. I was telling myself that Ontonagon was a good choice after all when, as usual, the idea of good luck woke my counting monster. Of all the Goddamm mementos I'd brought back from 'Nam, the Goddammdest was the counting. This time I found myself counting a column of snow-capped parking meters. The meters suggested a squad of helmeted grunts, which might have explained why I was counting, but it's just as likely the counting comes first and the meaning is tacked on. The brain can fool you like that – turn nothing into something, make it seem important. Stare long enough at the swarming flakes in a snow globe or the wriggling backdrop of a jungle, and phantoms appear, things loaded with personal meaning like messages from on high. And why not? You can't see nothing, can you? 'Nothing' is invisible. The brain imagines what it knows.

Thus, relevant or not, my mission for that go-round was to count expired meters. One, two, three – I called myself every species of asshole – four, five, six – but if words were all it took, the government would have saved a gunship or two on my Veterans Hospital bill – seven, eight, nine … *ten.* Ten is one *royally* fucked number. Ten wasn't working for me *at all,* so I bailed into a brightly lighted Rexall.

Shrugging my seabag, I stood just inside the door stamping snow from my boots and massaging my blue hands to get the blood flowing. A shaggy-haired counter clerk, my age, sized me up as something the wind blew in and went back to his stroke-book.

Ontonagon had been Don's choice for our hitchhiking trek. He'd lived there until he was five and remembered the nearby State Park from happy times with his Dad. Mainly we kept to the campground, however, case-hardening ourselves for the Corps with scorching, fly-bitten hikes through deep woods and icy dips in Superior. The town itself had been a mere side trip – one lazy wander-through we took the afternoon we left. Don said everything looked smaller and shabbier. The sight of his old house made him cranky.

Leaving my seabag standing crookedly like the Cat in the Hat's hat, I tramped over to the revolving paperback rack. For a moment I thought the books in the rack were the same ones I had shopped on my way out of town two years earlier. Nutty thoughts were getting easier for me to corral, so that one stayed put. *Actions,* however, still jumped the fence now and then. When I spun the rack, the gap of an empty slot reminded me of a missing-man flyby, and – like *that!* – I'm *counting* again. One slot, two slots … all the Goddamm way to fifty. The VA Docs had worked miracles on me, but I still felt itchy catching a number ending in zero. A do-over landed me a forty-nine, which was a keeper.

Two years back, while Don thumbed through a new *Road and Track*, I had pounced on a Spillane I hadn't seen, *The Long Wait*. Although I regularly had *some* book stuffed in my pocket, a new Spillane or Donald Hamilton or a new James Bond was like a letter from a lost friend and I let out a whoop. Don was unmoved. For him, *all* books were schoolwork, and Don's school days were over. Myself, I was eager to try college after the Corps. It puzzled me sometimes how different we were; more like *real* brothers, an accident, than blood-brother friends, a choice. Nudging him with my elbow, I picked up a *Playboy*.

The clerk *that* day had been a wispy, brown-haired, brown-eyed girl in glasses – probably my age, just out of high school, or perhaps still looking forward to senior year, blind to the fact that it might be her *best* year or even her last. I mean, downers like that don't usually grab you until later – a *lot* later if you're lucky.

I remembered her hair because it was cut short – shorter than Don's, almost as short as mine. I remembered particularly those forgettable brown eyes and how they watched my grubby fingers fondle the *Playboy*. Hoping to convince her I wasn't a pervert, I fussed over the cover, trying to sell Don on the interview and an article about the war. I also pointed out the hidden bunny in the cover photo, an earring that time. I was good at such detail, *too* good sometimes, witness my counting problem. Don snatched the magazine and yanked out the centerfold. That was Don – open book and strictly big picture. After 'Nam he hoped to race Formula One cars, a neat trick in Saginaw, but he accused me of nitpicking.

At the register I found myself mired in the clerk's boggy, brown eyes and my reflection in her glasses. Paying for the Spillane, two Mrs. Wagner's pies, the *Playboy*, and a pack of Winston's, I fumbled a handful of change. Don laughed and laughed harder when I slugged him in the arm.

He thought he knew why I was flustered since mental boners are baseline for teenage boys, particularly those whose home run reach had so far exceeded a few third base grasps. The story had a man-bites-dog twist to it, however, because my fantasy wasn't about sex.

Okay, maybe I *had* pictured the wispy girl naked – showering, I think, who remembers – but the point is, it wasn't sex that fixed me in the moment, because in the daydream we were just talking. And it wasn't what she said, because she was talking about nothing. The *weather*, I think!

What anchored me was a scent. A late-August scent. That sneezeless, fresh-air smell squeezed between a flowery Spring and a musty fall. That *clean* scent free of both pollen and mold because everything has fruited and nothing has yet died.

Maybe I was smelling a trace of the girl's shampoo or even imagining the scent, just as I was imagining her butt-naked weather report. Regardless, the fragrance rattled me, and suddenly, in the way you know something unsaid in a dream, I knew that I was staying. Or rather, I was fantasizing that I knew that I was staying.

It sounds jumbled because it was. I wasn't staying with the wispy clerk, or in town, or staying anywhere in particular. What it was, was that I wasn't *going*, not enlisting, which was my bright idea to begin with after Don caught a bad number in the draft lottery. *We'll go together, Don. Go Marines!* Those words had answered all our questions about the future.

I was so shook by Don's laugh and how silly I must have looked socking him and the crazy notion that he or the wispy girl would guess my goofy thoughts that I rushed outside and forgot my change. But I took an *idea* with me, one that

I saved – the idea that I had *chosen* to go and I could choose to stay. It's a losing-your-cherry moment when it finally penetrates that you *really can* choose things, that – while not exactly a do-over – every second *does* offer a choice to recast your future, even if only by choosing to upset the checker board when you know you can't win. And the topper was grasping that *'can't-choose-to-win'* part; realizing how much I *couldn't* choose; seeing that I could stay or go, but I couldn't do both; understanding that each choice was linked to earlier choices.

Back then I would have compared those links to the progression of a plot in a good book, but that's crap. If the connections are like those in a book at all, the book is one of those gimmicky kids' books, the kind where scrambled chapters end with numbered choices directing you to different pages.

1) Stay and marry the princess. Turn to page 52 *(where you think you'll live happily-ever-after).*
2) Sail away. Turn to page 107 *(where you hear the Siren).*

Choose and see what happens. Choose
not to choose and something happens
anyway. Pretend you have no choice.
That's a choice, too, another new chapter.

*Are* we captains of our souls?
Absolutely. But masters of our fate is
stretching it. The harbor we reach is
sometimes a long haul from the course
we plotted, because storms, and
doldrums, and monsters intervene. Ask
Odysseus.

Many of my ideas had spoiled in two years.
This one had lasted, although time had left it as
dry and bitter as a C-rat cracker. After all,
choices can be Goddamm meager sometimes, like
the choice to suffer or die. Sometimes they're as
hard to see as an ambush or as desperate as
hiding behind an elephant ear leaf. Sometimes
the only *immediate* choice seems to be the basic
one: eyes open or eyes closed. Eyes open buys you
the possibility of possibilities. Beyond that, you
get a choice to fight or flee or surrender to the
outcome of things, which – save for that game-
over choice – you *can't* choose, because you can't
do what you can't do, and you don't know what

you don't know, and the links of all your other choices are sometimes *chains*, and sometimes your heart overrules your head, and sometimes your timing is off, and sometimes you just have bad luck.

Still, you choose.

That's something you can count on. And things to *really* count on are not that hard to count.

Marveling at how a wispy girl had stuck with me – wham, bam, thank you ma'am – I spun the paperback rack and watched the books turn into a blur just as the books I kept in my head had become a blur.

"Say, do you want to buy a book?" said the clerk.

"I don't read anymore," I said, grabbing the whirling rack. Onetwothreefourfive books had spilled. "Tell me something," I said, replacing the onetwothreefourfive fallen books. "A girl worked here. Two years ago. Wispy-looking. She smelled … I dunno, hard to explain … Good, I guess. She smelled good. She still here?"

"I don't know," said the clerk.

"She wore a yellow sun dress."

"Let's hope she changed it."

I choked on a laugh. "Nothing gold can stay!"

The hippie-haired pogue's dumbass stare tickled me even more. "It's a joke," I spluttered. "A joke on a poem. I *used* to read."

The clerk's face soured as if he had a dicey choice to make. Perhaps he thought he should make me stop laughing, but the idea of him booting me out the door had me howling like the wind because you can't do what you can't do and you don't know what you don't know. The little clerk knew narrow schoolyard scuffles that ended with a cheek in the dirt and someone whining uncle, while I chose from a wide *world* of possibilities.

Sometimes my thoughts flowed like tree sap and other times they splattered and rolled every which way like balls of spilled mercury. When it registered that the clerk was backing away from me, I closed my eyes and took a deep breath.

"Sorry, buddy. I'm a little screwy from riding a bus all day," I said, opening my eyes and extending my empty hand. "I just got out of the hospital."

He shook hands reluctantly, but looked relieved that my laughter had stopped.

"Hospitals are bummers," he said. "I had my tonsils out once. What's up with you?"

"Post-Traumatic Stress Disorder."

"What's that?"

"You don't know what PTSD is?"

"Nope."

Bingo! Right where I needed to be. I almost threw my arm around the clerk's shoulders to noogie his shaggy head.

"New words for old, palie-pal, so maybe there's a genie, right?"

"Uh … got me, man."

"First it was shell shock, see? Then they called it war neurosis. Then combat fatigue. Get it?"

He shrugged.

"All *two* words, dig? PTSD is *four* words."

His face was blank. The guy's brain was blocking traffic. I tried a jump start.

"*Even* numbers … ?"

"I'm not following you."

"*Follow me* is an Army motto. *Semper Fi* is Marines, and I was a Marine. PTSD is what both bring back from 'Nam like the hard clap."

Even in a boonie-ville like Ontonagon, 'Nam was a direct hit. The look he gave me wasn't welcome home.

"I'm not a madman or anything," I said. "Skittish is all, and I don't sleep much. But look!" I pulled a purple ribbon from my pocket. "I won a prize at the fair."

"What fair?"

"Scarborough Fair."

"What's that supposed to mean?"

"I don't know," I said, scratching my head with the ribbon's bronze pendant. "I never understood it myself."

"That's a medal, isn't it?"

"Purple heart." I rubbed the pendant between my thumb and fingers like a worry bead.

"You don't take much care of it," said the clerk.

"No?" I smoothed the ribbon. "Well … I like to feel it in my pocket. Always there like a key. And, see, here's the thing. Say you raise a pet."

"I'm allergic. I don't have any pets."

"Just go with it, man. I'm trying to school you. Okay, say it's … say it's a goat. You allergic to goats?"

"Don't know. Never had one. A friend of mine has a lamb. That never caused a problem."

"... fucking mental war of attrition ..." I muttered. "Okay, great, we're getting somewhere. We'll say it's a lamb. You raise your lamb and take it to the fair where, sure enough, it wins a ribbon. That's good. But it's bye-bye lamb, hello mutton. That's bad. So you're ambivalent about your ribbon. The VA Docs eat that ambivalent word right up. Ten Goddamm letters, too, can you *believe* it? Count 'em. Ambivalent."

"I'd take care of it if I was you."

"Perhaps you're not ambivalent."

"You could get a clear case or something."

"I wouldn't feel it that way."

"Yeah, but you could still see it through the plastic."

"Like a snow globe?"

"Yeah. Like that."

Suddenly I was done with the clerk. I stuffed the ribbon back in my pocket.

"Hey, uh ... your face is kinda ... Are you okay, man?"

"I'm a cluster fuck," I said, shouldering my seabag. "Remember me to the girl who lives here."

"Who's that?" he said.

A jump start was hopeless. I opened the door to an icy blast, shielded my face behind my seabag, and leaned into the wind. Counting dark doorways instead of expired meters got me all the way to Lake Street. An ice-gripped dock notched a gap in a windbreak of storefronts and flats. The blizzard wailed through the gap as if issued from that very spot.

Once again, things were polar from what I remembered. I recalled that crossroad from a summery, Sunday afternoon, a lazy, Labor Day weekend that left two hitchhikers trolling a dried up traffic stream. A fruitless half-hour had put my ass on the curb and my back against a red fireplug. I think I smoked a cigarette and peeked at the Playboy, but the elements of the moment that stuck were sounds – a harmony of whispering breezes, rustling leaves, tapping branches, cawing gulls, peeping sparrows, buzzing bugs, barking dogs, a tinkling piano, fluttering flags, banging doors, and running through all of it, the undertone of my breath – a hollow, rising rush and falling sigh like the sound of something barreling toward me and speeding away.

Thumb outstretched to an empty road, Don circled a dozen yards back and forth. The dead stillness of the town had made him antsier than usual and usual was pretty antsy. School counselors called him hyperkinetic, a big, whistle-in-the-dark word that probably felt as good to them as ambivalent did to the VA Docs.

"Goddammit, I'm done with this place," he said. "Let's start walking."

"I'm not traipsing miles for nothing just because you're pissed about your old house. Any car down that road has to pass here."

Don made a show of almost spitting on my foot, then grabbed his pack and stamped across the street. He disappeared through a door beneath a sign that read Harbor Bar. I took my time, but I stood, hoisted my own pack, and followed.

Inside, Don was drumming his fingers on the bar and swiveling his squeaky barstool. I dropped my gear and slid onto a stool beside him.

The bartender – customers called him Hansen – let us stew, which was fine by me, because the place was cool and dusky and still.

Finally Hansen moseyed down the bar and planted himself in front of us. "I suppose you boys left your ID in your other pants, right?" He was short but thick with a bulldog jaw. His crossed forearms were covered with tattoos including a green eagle-globe-and- anchor.

"Give us a break, man," Don said. "We're Marines, too!"

"Not with *that* hair."

"Tuesday. We go in Tuesday. Soon as we catch a ride home."

Hansen flashed us a peace sign.

"Boot camp Tuesday night. You know what *that's* like. You gonna send us off without raising a beer? What's one stinking beer to a brother Marine?"

Hansen smiled at me and said, "Persistent little turd, ain't he?" He rubbed his tattoos as if they itched and sighed. "Look, boys, the Liquor Control don't miss a trick around here. They draft kids like you for tunnel rats. Send 'em in to flush out the fuck-ups. Still, considering the

times, I'd give you a beer, *if* you was Marines.
Thing is, until you *finish* boot camp, you're still
just pogues."

I asked him what a pogue was. Hansen said,
"Find out and come back. We'll have a round on
me. Promise."

That promise, I told myself, was why my teeth
were chattering in a blizzard when, twelve hours
earlier, I was rattling my hospital bunk with
shakes of a different sort. See, the V.A. pills were
like a side effect lottery. Blurred vision, cotton
mouth and brain fog were everyday, try-again
free tickets. Play routinely, however, and odds
were good for a Grand Prize – say, spasms that
twisted your body like a Gumby. For that, you
got more pills. Eventually all those pills left you
so wormy inside you couldn't stop moving. Your
legs jounced and your hands shook. Constantly!
To piss without sharing, you had to *sit*. And since
*no one* on a V.A. psych ward suffered without the
many, many benefits of the pills, other bunks
were rattling, too, while patients too spastic for
horizontal were shambling single-file up and
down the dead-end hallway. Almost goosey
enough to join *that* forlorn hope, I flashed on a

black-and-white, late-show scene – shuffling
P.O.W.s herded from Bataan. The image jolted
me like a grenade does when it's close enough to
get you, but doesn't. Suddenly, I'm hearing
myself say right out loud –

*Get up and go, man. Now. I mean now!
Do something. Choose something. Pick
another page. Go find a kiss for your
boo-boos or some chicken soup or a
toddy for your tummy. Choose
something. Anything. Anything else,
because* **this** *chapter is fucked. End of
story, man.* **This** *way is the exit.*

So, like that, I sign myself out against medical
advice – AMA they called it ominously as if the
A's were scarlet – and I'm counting down twelve
heebie-jeebie hours on a Greyhound bus to collect
the antidote of a three-year old IOU. And why
not? I knew what a pogue was. I even had
tattoos. Maybe not as pretty as Hansen's, but
just as indelible. And having become a true
believer in the sacrament of alcohol, I figured I'd
collect Don's drink, too. Waste not, want not. He
also served who only stood and waited.

If life *is* like a gimmicky kids book, *Waiting* was an apt title for the chapter Don flipped to when different choices out of boot camp finally took us separate ways. I was off to 'Nam while Don picked *school* of all things! Radio school. Afterwards, in its Green wisdom, the Corps assigned him garrison duty at Guantanamo Bay, Cuba – half a world away from the war.

Choices can be chains, and garrison duty is a tedious read. The pages are numbered in Mickey Mouse months of spit-shined shoes, polished buckles, inspections, and parades. I never understood how the days might be too many to count, but they weren't my days, and, besides, Don was hyperkinetic and lousy at detail. His letters suggested that he kept losing track.

A bad chapter doesn't kill you, however. It makes for a sloppy read and a hasty choice, but the choice kills, not the chapter. Don's choice was one I called deep powder. In over his head, he froze to death mid-summer in the tropics.

Waiting.

Dangling over the Lake Street crossroad, a blizzard-buffeted traffic signal yo-yoed wildly, showing first a red face, then green, then red

again. Whirlpools of loose snow swirled across
the crusted surface of deep snow. Crouching
against a fusillade of flakes, I charged for the lee
shelter of the Harbor Bar. In the front window, a
sign read: Help Needed.

I knew the feeling.

A chubby man tugging a fur-lined, parka-hood
over his head barged from the bar and waddled
away. I squeezed through a double-door vestibule
and stood waiting for my snow blindness to pass.

Although the vestibule muffled the storm, I
could still hear and feel its fury through the
walls and windows. It made me think of how it
was in country when a man broke down. How the
docs yanked him out of action, but only so far.
How they kept him close enough to hear and feel
the rumbles of shelling so he wouldn't forget how
real it was, all of it real, even the imagined parts
real in the way imagined things *are* real. How
the daily rain of mortar thumps and Howitzer
booms was like a sonic bath that scrubbed and
debrided the man's charred, contaminated soul,
kept it from scabbing and festering, enabled the
still-living part to scar and heal – or so the story
went.

I took a deep breath. The toasty barroom air – redolent of beer and smoke – was just as delicious as the air-conditioned air had been the first time I was there. I liked the Harbor all over again, and, once more, I wanted to stay.

Realizing he couldn't finagle a beer that end-of-summer day, Don had itched to hit the road. Glancing impatiently at a clock while I nursed a Coke at the bar, he busied his hands caroming a cue ball around the pool table. My cigarette burned down in a black ashtray. The gray ash lengthened and sagged.

"Let's stay," I said.

Don trapped the cue ball in a fist. "What?!"

"Let's stay. If not here, someplace else."

"Stay *home*?"

"No, not Saginaw. But somewhere. We don't have to go. We haven't signed anything yet."

"Are you a madman? Enlisting was your Goddamm choice from the get-go. We're all set."

I tried to explain what I had felt at the drugstore with the wispy clerk.

"You *are* nuts! ... Listen, Marlow, *you* have choices. Your number is a good one, you can wait and see. Or go to college and draw another

number, another time. War might be over by
then. Me? I can choose when, Tuesday, and how,
Marines." He plunked the cue ball onto the table
and stooped to hoist his pack. "You're not my
keeper, blood-brother. Go fuck your wispy clerk,
and while you're at it—"

"Pull yourself together, man!" I said, stubbing
out my smoke. "I was just saying, okay? Let's go."

A boozy old man in a madras sport coat
blurted from a nearby stool that he was passing
through Saginaw on his way back to Detroit. He
said he sold engine gauges to auto parts stores.
He was leaving late because he hated traveling
solo about as much as he hated selling engine
gauges.

"We could share the driving," he said. "Keep
each other company."

A little dab of Brylcreem had plastered slats of
red hair across the top of his pink, freckled dome.
He was drinking beer, but his breath smelled of
Wint-O-Green Lifesavers, the kind that make
blue sparks in your mouth if you crunch them in
a dark closet.

"I also have a case of Stroh's in an ice chest,"
he added with a wink.

Don was hooked, but I steered him aside, whispering that the guy looked flakey. He fumed that a ride all the way home was freak luck and that with two of us together, we wouldn't go wrong. He said I was stalling, called me another name or two. It wasn't worth letting him go it alone – which, given his rotten mood, he would have – so we tossed our packs in the salesman's station wagon. I crawled into the cargo space and stretched out among black-leather, sample cases while Don took the wheel. Riding shotgun, our benefactor fished a sweaty bottle of Stroh's from a cooler and thrust it over the seat. I shook my head. He pried off the cap, chugged half the bottle, and passed it to Don.

Towns across the Upper Peninsula were sparse, mostly whistle stops linked by long, straight stretches of two-lane blacktop plowed through unchanging forest. Mile after monotonous mile, painful enough, was made *unbearable* by a barrage of locker-room talk from the salesman – an endless run-on sentence that comma-spliced *blowjobs*, and *doing it* and *tapping that young ass*. Sharing our boundless fantasy and circumscribed reality with an old pervert seemed sordid to me, but Don was game. Their drone lulled me to sleep until a screech of brakes slammed me into the seat back.

I felt the car shudder onto a gravel shoulder and slew to a stop. I jerked up and saw the salesman scrunched against the passenger door. Don jumped out, flung open the rear door and heaved our packs into the road. The look on his face scared me. The salesman looked scared, too, and I think he *was* scared, but he was also grinning. As soon as I scrambled out, he scooted under the steering wheel, floored the gas pedal, and spit gravel peeling away.

The setting sun had dropped below tree tops leaving the road in shadow. Silently Don and I dragged our packs onto the shoulder.

"So where are we?" I said finally.

Don looked back as if to see how far we had come.

"Past Ishpeming. Half-way to Mackinaw."

"Stuck in the doldrums," I sighed.

"You don't even have to ask what happened, do you, Mr. Wizard?"

I shrugged.

Don turned his back and jabbed out his thumb although, save for the vanishing dot of the station wagon, the road was empty.

An icy blast of wind cracked open the vestibule door and broke my reverie. I noticed a squad of seven old timers huddled around a table strewn with beer mugs.

"Don't be shy, sonny," one buddy cackled, flashing a toothless grin. "Nobody here but us chickens!"

They laughed, raised mugs, slapped knees, pounded the table. It's good to have buddies in a storm.

The barroom was a deep rectangle. A red-vinyl booth filled the front corner. A brightly lighted pool table and a glowing Wurlitzer occupied a rear alcove. In between were the long bar, vacant stools, and empty tables and chairs. I squeezed past the rowdy buddies, shuffled to the end of the bar, and shrugged my seabag.

Growing up I had felt at ease most everywhere because I had never *been* anywhere. That comfort was long gone, however. The buddies made me edgy – people who weren't *my* people in a place that wasn't *my* place. Realizing what a long-shot

I had played, I was anxious to spot Hansen. After all, the promise I was chasing was from another time and the calendar isn't changed when you forget what day it is. Gulping air and feeling wobbly, I grabbed hold of the bar and started to count liquor bottles.

When Hansen pushed through a swinging door, the relief I felt was a little like what I'd felt curled on a litter watching those crazy bastards in the Huey swooping toward the hot LZ. He shot me the *what's-your-story* look people give strangers, but caught the headline stenciled on my worn seabag and read the details etched in my face.

"Welcome home, Marine," he said.

*Good Goddamm words*!

"I, uh ... I had a buddy," I said, climbing onto a stool. "We stopped here a couple years back. On our way to boot camp. My buddy tried to con you out of a beer."

Wiping his gnarly-knuckled hands on a fresh, white towel, Hansen smiled. Perhaps my face had changed less than I thought.

"Sure! I remember. You and this hippie-haired pogue. I told you to come back when you weren't."

"I'm back."

Hansen brushed at his tattoos.

"Your buddy couldn't make it?"

I shook my head.

"Another time, maybe?"

I shook my head again.

"I owe you men, don't I?" Hansen said.

He turned  to fetch a dusty brown bottle – Hennessy – from the top shelf. He lined up three glasses and poured. Lifting one in a silent salute, he slugged back the shot and banged down the glass. I did the same. The third glass sat there. I picked it up when Hansen nudged it my way. It felt cold in my hand. Like snow.

 "Last man standing," Hansen said. "In the end, all you have are memories, and those you lose, too. Drink up."

I downed the shot and lowered the glass gently onto the bar. Hansen swooped up the empties and washed them clean.

"You were lucky to catch me today," he said. "I'm usually off Tuesdays, but my relief is snowed in so we switched. Tomorrow you would've missed me."

"*Guest Star* and *Anything Can Happen days*," I muttered.

He looked puzzled.

"Tuesday and Wednesday on the Mickey Mouse Club. It's nothing. I'm just thinking out loud."

"I do it all the time. Occupational hazard," he said, turning to his affairs.

The alcohol was a warm glow. I felt something inside me cracking like the frozen Saginaw River does when it starts to run again in Spring. Once more I thought about life as a jumbled kids' book and I thought about luck.

Luck isn't everything, that's for sure. Chance favors the prepared. You choose your best choice, knowing what you know, doing what you can, and you flip the pages, trusting to your wits. But you Goddamm *hope* for luck, knowing it's something you'll need in the long run because – if you're still standing on that new page, in that next chapter – you choose again and keep choosing until wits fail or the luck runs out.

Swiveling the stool to take in the bar – to make it *my* place, the buddies *my* people – I thought, "To lucky choices." Naturally, the thought of good luck spooked my counting monster, but, for a change, the numbers added up.

Onetwothreefourfive—

I mean, some sorry pogue covering for Hansen might have carded me, writing new choices and an unlucky ending for the chapter.

Sixseveneightnineten—

Because, despite all the validations stamped on me and in me, my years still numbered ten, count 'em, ten-Goddamm-ten, times two.

*Too young* to drink.

*Too young* to gamble.

*Too young* to buy a gun.

And, back then, too young to vote on any of it.

A whole world of evils and ten-Goddamm-ten, times two was too young for *almost* all of them.

## 2. FRIENDLY FIRE

So I'm ten days out of the VA, spending yet another fruitless afternoon dissecting the hospital discharge chit that says I'm finally squared away, only I'm counting commas for a change, hoping that some new count will finally add things up, when – POW! – right between the running lights it hits me that I'm still hidey-holed in my Goddamm room, and off I diddy-bop to Tiger stadium for a twi-night double header, where I'm camped in left field with my Cracker Jack and my soda, root-root-rooting for the home team, when I start to laugh at a joke so funny I damn near pop!

Yet despite its crystal, crystal clarity, those left field pogues aren't getting the joke *at all*, and

their numb-nuts bellyaching just sends soda
spraying out my pie hole and makes it so I can't
*stop* laughing until, finally, this one hippie dude
in a Wayne State jersey shrugs off his
yammering girlfriend to bust me smack in the
snot locker while onetwothreefourfive buddies
pile on like it's an oh-dark-thirty blanket party
for some platoon shitbird, all six of them jinking
around like Keystone Cops, slugging me, kicking
me, plain *wailing* on me, man! and it's funny, I
mean *boo-coo* funny, especially with my eyes
closed, because I can almost see this Chinese fire
drill from above, like I'm a big Cheshire grin on a
perch watching some home-team fan way down
below scrabble under seats so a squad of
friendlies can't stomp him, but surprise! Folding
seats, right? Haha!

I laughed and laughed, even when real cops
waded in with clubs to play a round of Whack-A
Mole on me, all of them good-natured enough
about it, since cops are birds of a feather, wise to
how much a uniform can cost a guy, and already
the grabass had lost me my white hat – rolled
away somewhere like a Johnny-cake – and left
my dress blues with torn pockets flapping, gold

buttons popped, a row of ribbons dangling by one pin, and popcorn and peanut shells stuck to me like lint to a lint roller.

Reluctant to cage a fallen, but kindred sparrow, the cops evak'd me instead to Receiving Hospital where I spent a wide-eyed night strapped to a gurney while humorless nurses pumped my ass full of some dolorous drug to make me stop laughing.

Mainly it made me cramp and squirm like a spade-cut worm.

That part *hurt*.

So I did stop laughing.

But you can't fool those sick-bay pogues. They bounced me back to the VA anyway. And for a long, *long* time afterward, I judged it politic to keep the joke to myself.

## 3. HEROES

Denny sat alone at the end of the bar, his usual stool in the corner. He slumped forward, weight resting on his elbows. One fist bolstered his head. The other fist clutched a beer mug. The blank TV screen seemed to enthrall him like a snake's eye does a bird. Shaking his head to break the spell, he tapped his mug.

Yawning, I ambled down the bar to draw his refill. It was early for me. With Hansen back in the hospital for his stomach cancer, I was covering both days *and* nights.

"See the fight, Marlow?" Denny said.

"Some fight," I snorted, pushing a fresh beer across the bar. "I saw a *crime*."

"Ever tell you I was in the ring once?"

"Go on, Denny!"

"God's honest truth, man!"

Denny was only thirty-something, my age, but he looked drained. He was tall, but bent, and gaunt in an empty way, like Hansen had become, gnawed from the inside by that hungry tumor. The bones of Denny's fingers were as thin as pencils. His skin was the color of used china. I couldn't picture him mixing it up in a ring.

"Fought a *behemoth*, Marlow. Like a monster you fight in dreams. It's a funny story. You'll laugh."

Denny's talk was always hollow talk. Never *about* anything. Never himself. Never the past. All I knew for sure was that he was single, despised the Tigers, and had come north from Detroit about fifteen years earlier to sell cars at Peninsula Ford, his uncle's lot. That wasn't much history and with Hansen so sick I *needed* a funny story. Wiping my hands, I stood waiting.

"Looking back, I can see I had the reach on him," Denny said. "I'm tall, right? But I was bones to his solid muscle. He had sandbag arms, knobby, scarred knuckles. His nose was bent and his scalp was shiny smooth with thick folds in back. He struck you as slow, but he could catch a buzzing fly with either hand.

"We were both Motor City boys. I was twenty, he was eighteen. His name was ... I forget, some dumb Polack name. Kanowsky, maybe. We fought in San Diego at the boot camp where I spent the summer of '68 after joining the Corps."

"*Get out!*"

"Caught you off guard, didn't I, Marlow? Me a Marine, just like *you*."

"Most men mention it, Denny."

"*Tell* me about it! Well, guess what? With all the *losers* in that club, membership isn't something I advertise. Take this Kanowsky, for instance. Before the Corps he was a high-school dropout doing bedpans at Detroit General Hospital, because – get this! – someone had cracked open his head during the riots and the hospital glued it back together. He offered that a week in the hospital taught him all he needed to know – some punch-drunk notion that, working for the hospital, even losers are good guys, because they're part of a *team* doing good. That's just the way he put it. Good guys doing good. The big goon was so stoked by this brainstorm, he hired on at the hospital until he turned eighteen, when – you guessed it! – he up and joined a *'better'* team. Yeah, right! A few good men, my ass. A few losers and boozers and silly bastards who wanted to be heroes."

"Which were you?"

"You want me to tell this or not?"

Denny was hard to like, but I wanted to hear his story, so I piped down.

"Funny thing, Marlow," he said after a pause. "I had it made back then. Four walls near the campus. A solid, C-average 2-S deferment. A student loan and an allowance from Mom. Who pisses that away? Tell me, who? *No* one, that's who! But I did! Just pissed it away the night I decided to enlist."

He shook his head. "How does it happen, something like that? You do something, and I guess you choose to do it, so it's in you to do it, but it's like ... I don't know, it's like those times when hail falls on a clear summer day. It's hot as blazes and suddenly ... *ice*. Some things, there's no explaining, I guess.

"So let's just say, once upon a time – a little frazzled since school was making me choose a major – I watched *Sands of Iwo Jima* on the late show and next day found myself listening to this rock-jawed Marine Corps recruiter. You know the type – gold-button dress-blues, a chest-full of hero medals, the white hat with that spit-shined visor you can see yourself in. And, naturally, he had the eagle, globe, and anchor on his arm. Like Hanson has. Like, I bet, *you* have somewhere, too. You *all* have one, my old man sure did. I hardly remember his face – I was barely off the tit when he joined up and got himself killed at Chosin Reservoir – but damned if I don't remember that tattoo. Anyway, a few nights later I'm in boot camp, crying in my pillow."

I laughed.

"See, Marlow? Funny! But we're not all the same stuff, man. Maybe *you* didn't imagine it one way, then see it all change like summer to winter in one night.

"The dozen of us from Detroit – rowdy enough on the plane – were straightaway cowed by D.I.s who met us at the airport. They herded us outside into a waiting transport and ordered us not to move or make a sound and no one, I mean *no one*, did. The truck lumbered away, circled around the airport to the recruit depot, and shuddered to a hissing-brakes stop. The doors clattered open and – man-oh-man! – the *world* caved in. D.I.s were growling and snarling; stalking, pouncing, mauling. Every word was repeated, repeated. Every word SHOUTED! They pressed into you, chest to chest. You couldn't fight, you couldn't flee! You *froze*. Mouth parched, palms wet, eyes wide and blinking. Stripped, shorn, sweating bodies squeezed together. The smell, Marlow. That *smell!*

"It was a ... a fever dream! I endured it in the naked light, what else could I do? But when finally they granted us an hour of sleep near dawn, I hugged that single privacy, darkness, pressed my face into my pillow, and *bawled* until – Christ, I almost pissed myself! – I  felt a hand on my shoulder."

"'You're that college guy, ain't you?' whispered a voice from the next rack, a blabbermouth I recognized from the plane, Kanowsky. 'It's okay, man. It's okay. Hard choice, cryin' in your pillow, 'stead of just boo-hooin' so everyone sees you like some done. You're a good man. Hang in there. We'll all get through this together.'"

"Patting my back like you'd pat a baby, he rolled over, squeaked the springs settling in, and was snoring in minutes.

"I hated him, Marlow! Some meathead bucking for Chaplain! I hated his tone, his ... his touch. I hated him being so Goddammed *close* to me. Oh, Marlow, Marlow. It was a *very* long summer.

"Not the least of it was timing. '68 was the year of the Tigers, remember? Denny McLain? Mickey Lolich? Those names *still* raise goosebumps. And there I was, a Detroit boy, missing it all. Funny how McLain crapped out afterwards, but shit happens, I guess. He still had his season. You can't take that season away, can you?"

"You hate the Tigers, Denny."

He swirled the beer in his mug. "Yeah ... yeah, I guess I do." He took a drink.

"But the worst part, Marlow, was the attitude. And not just the D.I.s. *Everyone* there had an attitude. Everyone, that is, but Big Daddy Kanowsky. Christ, he *adopted* me. 'We oughta work together, man,' he said, no matter how I insulted him. 'You got brains most of us don't. Help us with the bookwork. We're on the same team.'"

"Can you believe it? Me on *his* team? Cleaning the crappers? A sacrament to Kanowsky. Physical training? Flat out every time. Obstacle course? Flat out, as if his life depended on it. I used to snicker at him poring over the Marine Corps Manual, his lips moving. All he said was 'we oughta work together.'

"The day he exploded was hot with a hot wind. Maybe the dust from the weight training pit finally got to him as it had me, an itchy, yellow dust that tickled your throat so you coughed all night."

Denny paused to take another long drink.

"Were you at Parris Island or San Diego, Marlow?"

For an instant my ears felt sunburn prickly and my lungs leathery from coughing.

"A Hollywood Marine," I said.

"Then you remember that dust. Christ! How do they expect a man to lift when he can't *breathe*? I was curling 60 pounds at one station, while across from me, Kanowsky bench-pressed a bar bowed by several train wheels on each end – maybe 300 pounds. His face was red and wet; his temple veins bulged. I muttered something offhand – I lift your IQ, you lift mine – nothing more than he always shrugged off, but something popped. Maybe one of those veins. He crashed his weights back onto the stand, sprang up, and slammed me against a hooch, snarling, 'I'm sick of you! You don't belong here!' His eyes were slits. Saliva bubbled in the corners of his lips. He pinned me squealing to the wall and cocked his right fist."

"'He jumped me!' I gasped to Gunny Brown as three D.I.s piled into Kanowsky and pried him off me. 'Shut your hole, College Puke!' the Gunny growled. Kanowsky shook himself free and snapped to attention. The Gunny eyed us silently. A hot gust swirled a tiny dust devil across the pit. 'Settle it in the ring,' the Gunny said finally."

"'B..but he'll annihilate me!' I sputtered."

"The Gunny shot me a tobacco-stained grin. 'Well, that's some up to *you* now, isn't it?'"

"Marching the platoon to the vacant gym – a corrugated-metal, hangar building, oven-hot like a tin-roofed shed – Gunny Brown ordered Kanowsky and me into a boxing ring while the rest of the unit clumped over a section of bleachers.

'You'll *kill* me, man!' I pleaded to Kanowski under my breath.

"He stuck his chin in my face and said, 'What do you care? You don't love nothin'. You don't respect nothin'. You don't *feel* nothin'. Well, *this* you're gonna feel. This'll be real, real for keeps. Make a choice, pogue.'"

"'I can't win!' I spluttered."

"He looked surprised. *Really* surprised. 'You mean, college don't learn you that—'"

"I didn't hear the rest because floodlights blazed on overhead, sparking hoots from the platoon at my baggy sweatshirt and tight shorts. When I started to protest again, Gunny Brown shushed me with a Listerine-tasting, rubber mouthpiece crammed between my teeth. Lacing cracked, red gloves on my hands, he secured the lace ends with bandage tape while Sergeant Butts finished with Kanowsky and stepped out of the ring. Staying to referee, the Gunny nudged Kanowsky and me toward opposite corners with a 'Good luck, men.' D.I.'s *never* called us men.

"I was petrified. Nothing I could remember had *ever* been worth fighting for. Across the ring Kanowsky slapped his fists together and flicked a thumb at his nose. The light glinted off his ugly, bald head. His eyes gleamed. He snorted, danced, fired combos into the padded turnbuckle.

"A bell clanged. Kanowsky charged at me. I flung my hands out and tried to weasel around him, but he moved inside, backed me against the ropes, bobbed a little to the right, and snapped a left jab into to my face.

"A flashbulb went off and my lower lip popped open, I mean *popped*, like a squished grape. Tear blinded, I swung wildly, but, close inside, Kanowsky sloughed off the roundhouses and nailed me with that left. Two more tags, I clutched my neck and took a dive.

"Kanowsky just stood there looking down at me. Now that's failure to take a corner, right? Theoretically I scored a point, right? Practically speaking, however, it was pretty clear that getting up wasn't on my to-do list."

"'College ain't learned you nothin' you need to know,' Kanowsky declared finally. The last I ever saw of him was the gold USMC on his red sweatshirt as he stooped through the ropes and disappeared into the darkness beyond the ring lights."

"So, that's it?" I said. "That's the big fight?"

"Yeah, Marlow, that's the fight. What did you expect?"

"Maybe a *fight*?"

"Wait!" he blurted, grabbing my sleeve as I turned. "I mean, uh … wait. I'm not to the funny part yet. See, I had a ballooned up eye and nose, a split lip, and as far as anyone knew from my wailing, a broken neck – maybe enough to finagle a light-duty day from some green corpsman at sick-bay. But when Gunny Brown yelled for an ambulance and knelt to brace my neck with rolled towels, I sensed a concern unlikely to be for me. At the hospital a Red Cross lady confirmed it; making me fight like that was *illegal*. I sneaked a collect call to Mom who hired a lawyer and, Marlow, I *won*. General discharge, good of the service.

"I had to wait, of course. Spent months in the casual platoon with the fuck-ups and the feebs. The spiteful bastards refused to let me go until October – *two stinking weeks* before I qualified for veterans' benefits. Yeah, right!

"And when I *did* make it home, all that San Diego sunshine must've bleached my brain, because I felt like an *alien*. How *gray* Detroit looked. How red-cheeked cold it felt. How sour the burning leaves smelled. I'd never noticed that before.

"But the *big* shock was the Tigers. Remember? Down three, they took three straight to win the Series. First time since '45.

"Man, what a scene! Detroit was one, giant party. Horns blaring like bugles, strangers kissing in the streets, confetti blowing like snow in the wind. People were hugging, dancing, laughing, cheering – and I'm talking whites and blacks *together*, man. Barely a year since rioters torched half the city, and suddenly everyone's on the same team."

He fell silent for a moment.

"It was weird though. I was *right there*, downtown in the thick of things, but ... Oh,  I dunno. I guess if you miss the season, you can't be part of it. I mean, I couldn't *feel* any of it." He shook his head. " ... Goddamm heroes ..."

Another pause.

"Winter came on fast after that, and I never got around to school. Mom finally wheeled a job out of my uncle, but just before I moved up here, I read about Kanowsky's homecoming. A gushy

*Free Press* spread. Pictures of a dress-blue
Captain handing his Mom and Dad a box of
medals and a flag. For what? We still lost, right?
*He* lost! He's dead. And for what? Answer me
that. For what? I'm supposed to feel something
for the Goddammed hero?"

I looked at the clock.

"You're late, Denny."

"Late? Yeah, sure, I'm late. What's the dif?
Who's buying cars these days? I'm lucky to
squeak by. And besides, Marlow, you still haven't
heard the *funny* part.

"You know how sometimes you look back – like
you're rewinding your life, replaying some part?
You do that, right? Everyone does that, right? ...
Well, the funny thing is that the worst moment
in my life has become the only one that I can
actually feel. I *feel* the tiny needles of grit
pricking my scraped cheek pressed flat against
the canvas. I *taste* the salty blood in my mouth,
*smell* my own fear sweat, *hear* the stomping feet
on the bleachers as I squint into the lights at
that hero Kanowsky. It's so *real* to me! So alive.
It's like I can still *do* something. Still make some

choice. But what? I can't fight the fight again, can I? But it's like I can still make a choice.

"What, Marlow? What choice? The fight is *over*, man, so what choice am I supposed to make? *What choice*? No! I did the *smart* thing, man, and – Goddamn it! – I'd do it *again*."

Abruptly a spark in him that I hadn't seen before fizzled.

"And there's the funny part, Marlow. How the catcalls and the glare and the prickly cheek and the salty taste all vanish when I think that. And not just *those* feelings, but *feelings*. It's like I'm numb again until the next time. Funny, huh?"

He laughed, but it wasn't a funny laugh.

I didn't know what to say, but I had to say something, so I tried to make it a joke. "You cudda been a contender, pogue."

He upended his beer, slapped down a few dollars, and faltered toward the door and the daylight.

"Once," he said, not looking back. "Once upon a time."

## 4. THE GAMES

*I have sinned exceedingly, in thought,*
*word and deed: through my fault,*
*through my fault, through my most*
*grievous fault.*

*The Confiteor*

"Eight hammers!" whooped the Polack, bursting from a tunnel that connected the locker room to the arena.

"That's a Goddamm good bit," said a whiskered, old-timer playing cards at a rickety card table.

A fortyish woman sitting opposite the old man discarded a black ten. "He's breaking your balls, George. Who does eight hammers?"

The woman spat tobacco juice into a tableside bucket. The old man nodded.

The locker room was a cinderblock box buried beneath the grandstand, a windowless limbo permeated with an ageless musk of oiled leather, rosin, foot powder, and wintergreen liniment. A tiled archway led to a bank of hissing showers. Steam clouds wafted through the archway and rolled across the corrugated metal ceiling. The clouds formed wavering haloes around wire-caged bulbs and beads of condensation along exposed pipes. The crystal beads swelled, ripened, fell, and recurred. Tall, gray, wall lockers surrounded the room like a phalanx of soldiers.

Waiting players, clothed and unclothed, lolled on wooden benches, kibitzed around the card table, lighted and left from folding chairs scattered around a television monitor. A bare-assed teenager, towel-drying his shaggy hair, padded in from the showers.

"Cripes, eight hammers! Did he make it?"

A jock-strapped player, lounging with his back against a locker, lifted a hand-towel draped over his face to shade his eyes from the lights. "Get wise, newbie."

"Fifty-two yards! I watched from the tunnel," said the Polack. "He fumbled a pair when he went down, but—"

"That's a deduction," scoffed the lounger.

The Polack wheeled as if to charge. He was a big man whose bulging shoulders and legs strained the seams of his gray business suit.

"Someone die and make you a judge, pal? It was a Goddamm good bit, hear me? Best I ever saw. Ever!"

The lounger yawned and let his towel drop.

"Eight and fifty-two might just be a record for Hammers," mused the old card player, mouthing a soggy cigar.

"Wait for the points," said the lounger through his towel. "Without the points you're pushing your pud."

Miming a puckered 'wait for the points' expression, the newbie snatched at the draped towel. The lounger seized the newbie's wrist and held it like a cobra caught by a mongoose.

"That's a yellow card, kid. One to a customer."

"Okay, okay, leggo!" grimaced the newbie, jerking his arm free.

"Did you see who's on deck?" asked the old-timer.

"Fat Dolph," muttered the Polack, fingering a stethoscope that dangled from his thick neck.

"Was he wearing the white suit?"

"I don't know. Maybe ... Yeah, I think so."

The old timer drew a card. "He's doing Ducks, all right."

"Ducks is a laugher. I'd *never* do Ducks," snickered the newbie, massaging his wrist.

Abruptly the shower hiss grew louder and the boy wished there were do-overs. The fortyish woman rolled a tobacco cud from one cheek to the other and spat again.

"Dyin's easy," she said, flipping a card. "Comedy's hard."

"Look, I ... I ain't knockin' his bit or nothin'. His bit, his choice, right? I just meant Ducks ain't right for me, that's all. You know? For *me*."

Covering himself with the towel, the newbie retreated to his locker. He took out his shoes, straddled a bench, and made a show of picking at cleats. Beside him, a beefy man doing Drawings arranged mechanical pencils in a pocket protector.

"Excuse me, sir," said the newbie sheepishly. "Maybe you know what's what. Should I suit up or somethin'?"

"Hard to say. It's a mystery how names are called, but players usually have to sit a spell, so most wait. Take Liz, there ... the card player doing Babies? She waited a *long* time. Too long in my book. I mean, think about it. How long do you risk missing your turn? But now she's set, see? On the other hand, you have your Polack ... the big guy doing stethoscopes? He's been good to go from day one – suit, tie, the whole shebang. Man I bet that's misery for him, too. Probably why he's so antsy."

"Gotcha. Yeah, that's a help."

Silently the newbie scratched at a faint stain on one of his shoes.

"Some guys really sweat them arrows, don't they?" he said abruptly. "It can't hurt all *that* bad."

"Probably worse than the slings," grunted the beefy man, shrugging a heavy breastplate over his shoulders.

"Right on! Them slings just gotta be a laugher. And they say you're so stoked, you don't feel none of it no way. That's what they say."

"That's what they say, all right."

The newbie tugged at a cleat with his thumb and forefinger, then plunked the shoe back on the bench. "Only ... well, sometimes you see 'em, and, well, they're like, *squirmin'*, you know? You seen 'em, too, right? How sometimes they—"

"Those shoes cleaned up real good. You must be doing Words."

The newbie slumped forward, elbows on his knees.

"Words is my passion," he sighed. "Most times I got more mouth than sense."

"And iron legs, too."

The boy thumped a fist into his solid thigh. "Pretty good, I guess. So?"

The older man cinched a buckle on his breastplate.

"Words is a distance bit. First you have to last."

"There goes Fat Dolph!" announced the lounger, peeking at the monitor from beneath his towel. "It's a Duck bit, all right."

Fat Dolph was funny and friendly. The players all liked him. A dozen or so gathered around the screen and watched six white ducks skitter downfield while Fat Dolph, wearing a silly white outfit, waddled in pursuit. "Listen to 'em laugh," the newbie said hesitantly.

"Fans *love* Ducks," said the lounger. "Grab 'em, Dolph!"

"Head shot," winced a player. "Slings are dead-on today."

"Archers, too," observed a gangly player who lockered next to Dolph. "Lousy, lousy start," he said, walking away.

Blood from numerous wounds splotched Dolph's suit and any ducks he caught.

"Cripes, he can't hold 'em!"

"That's Ducks, newbie. A bloody duck is as slippery as soap."

Protesting wildly, the ducks squeezed from beneath Dolph's arms or wiggled from his hands, and, of course, each time he stooped for one – whammo! – another arrow.

"Gotta grip the legs," instructed the beefy man, demonstrating with a fist. "Grab those scaly feet and—"

"Look! He got 'em all!"

"By the legs, see? It's the only way."

"Oooo. Dead in the ticker. He's done."

"No, look!" exclaimed the newbie.

Fat Dolph staggered forward, his jelly-belly quaking, Gripping six ducks by their waggling feet, he raised his arms to heaven as if to ascend on their furiously flapping wings. The stands roared with delight long after Dolph fell. The watching players dispersed silently, however, ignoring the slo-mo highlights, commentary, reaction shots, and the stock buffoonery of the grounds crew rounding up ducks that had skittered away when Dolph's fingers uncurled.

"Never a long run with Ducks," remarked the beefy man returning to his locker. "Too much scatter."

"Eighteen yards!" insisted the newbie. "Eighteen's *great* for Ducks."

"Wait for the points, kid," the lounger said, lowering his towel over his face. "Without the points you got zip."

"Look, I ... I didn't mean nothin' 'bout Dolph when I said what I said," the newbie stammered. "Ducks is good. *Real* good." He raised his voice. "As good as ... as Hammers. Or Babies. Or Words or Songs. Or Dollars! They're *all* good. Laughers too! All good bits. Honest!" The boy felt foolish talking only to himself. His words tailed off. "Really. I, uh ... I didn't, you know ... mean nothin' then."

"Count on more newbies," the lounger muttered. "Every good bit we get a brood."

The newbie plumped onto the lounger's bench. "So what brought *you* down?"

"The stairs."

"Remember when I came?"

"Gee ... I'd have to check my notes."

"Cripes, I was still chewin' a hot dog. This player, Kemp, had did a Daddy bit and—"

"Kemp brought you down?" said the lounger, raising his towel.

"I remember Kemp," said the beefy man, carefully securing his pencil-filled pocket protector in the breastplate pocket. "Kemp did a good bit. A *damn* good bit!"

"I couldn't just sit no more. Couldn't just watch. Was it the same for you guys?"

The lounger's eyes gleamed. "The door from the stands swings both ways, kid. The waiting is already gnawing at you. Traipse another block or two down memory lane and you'll be hightailing it back."

"I'm a player!"

"You're *waiting* to be a player."

"Same as you! Same as all of us!"

"We hear that some newbies sneak back and do bits in the stands," said the lounger. "Like this peanut man we hear about who tosses peanut bags. Like a laugher."

"That ain't no bit! Tossin' peanuts around a shady stadium with a beer in your belly ain't no bit."

"Really? You think?"

"Yeah, I think!"

"Then take some free advice."

"Yeah? What free advice you got for me?"

"Stake out a comfy spot, kid. Sounds like you'll be here a while."

"Like me!" brayed the old card player. "Waiting till doomsday to do my bit."

His opponent flipped a discard face down and fanned her cards on the table. "Maybe Waiting *is* your bit, George."

The old man almost swallowed his soggy cigar. "Samson in pigtails, guys, she's got it! It's all making sense now. I'm doing *Waiting*." He threw in his cards, scraped back his chair, and hobbled over to the red, metal door marked 'EXIT.'

"That door locks behind you, George."

"Bite me, Liz. I need some air."

The old man cracked the door and peered outside. He peeled the wet cigar from his lips.

"In or out, George?" the woman said, sweeping the cards together.

The old man stared a moment more, then spat. "Still in," he said, chomping on his cigar stub and hitching back to the table.

A name resonated from an overhead loudspeaker.

"I'm up!" exclaimed the Polack. He sprang for the  tunnel, but stopped short. Yanking off his stethoscope, he hurried to the equipment bin, shed his coat and tie, and dragged out an umbrella-shaped deflecting mitt.

"No Stethoscopes?" remarked the beefy man doing Drawings. "Stethoscopes is a good bit."

"I'm doing Hammers!"

"He shouldn't oughta flip-flop like that," whispered the newbie. "Should he?"

"Some do," replied the beefy man, ambling toward the card table. "Kemp changed his bit, as I recall."

"That Kemp was good," muttered the lounger. "Did a good bit."

The Polack disappeared into the tunnel.

"I'm gonna watch," said the newbie.

The beefy man shrugged, sized-up the discards, and asked, "Who's winning?"

* * * * *

Sun-blinded as he exited the tunnel, the big Polack shielded his eyes and surveyed the hard-baked, black-and-white playing field. A frail-looking woman was doing Dustpans, a good bit. Faraway downfield, the end-zone shimmered like a mirage.

The big man loped toward the on-deck circle. The air was as dry as a rosin bag. Each breath rasped in his lungs. Already he missed the steamy amnion of the locker room.

Kneeling in a chalk circle strewn with equipment, he carefully crisscrossed his shoulders with pairs of massive sledgehammers joined by braided cords. Although the dangling hammerheads would pound him as he ran, they also served as armor against the stones and arrows. What to expose, what to protect, what to pound? Good choices made for a great bit.

A blaring klaxon cut short his preparations. He donned the deflecting mitt, struggled to his feet, and trudged toward the starting line. While judges tallied points, a silhouetted grounds-crew removed the Dustpan player and tidied the field. The scoreboard read one hundred seventy-six yards. *Excellent* for Dustpans.

The big man frowned. Dustpans, like Stethoscopes, was a distance bit; Hammers was strictly mid-field. While comparison was unfair, judges were all too human. Long yardage right before his own bit would surely cost him points. Why had he switched? *Why?!* Watching that eight-Hammer bit had been bad Goddamm luck.

Settling the five cords of the hammers with a final shrug, he spit in the direction of the judges' tower. Were points the point? Were yards the point? The *bit* was the point, a bit that swelled your heart and guts with pride, because, lacking *that,* playing was absurd. Allowing himself one sneering glance at the irrelevant stands, he lowered his head and buried the knuckles of his right hand in the white chalk of the starting-line.

His tongue was as dry as the chalk. His heart flapped like Fat Dolph's ducks. He was afraid, but also relieved. He was eager, and nevertheless sad that his bit would soon be done.

His feelings were familiar from countless *imagined* bits. Having always imagined Stethoscopes, however, he was surprised at how the feelings welled like the rush he had felt watching eight hammers, and *astounded* at how, this time, the feelings flooded and overflowed.

Of course, *this* time it was *his* Hammer bit.

And he was doing *ten.*

The starting gun cracked. Shielding his head in the crook of one elbow, he zigzagged downfield, deflecting whizzing arrows with the wide mitt. Stones peppered his back and legs and pinged off the bobbling hammer heads. The cords suspending the weighty hammers sawed into his shoulders while the swinging steel heads pounded his knees. A fire spread from his lungs to the muscles of his legs, his arms, his back. His vision blurred.

The pain of the first arrow, however, snapped the world into crystalline focus. Suddenly his limbs responded with an effortless syncopation to surprisingly simple rhythms in the whirling choreography of the Slingmen, the reciprocating dance of the Archers. The rain of stones and arrows was rendered a slow sprinkling. And since, luckily, the first arrow had pierced his free arm, unimportant in Hammers, his deflecting mitt batted aside the listless missiles like lazy balloons.

Oddly, however, the mitt grew heavy like a sponge absorbing a monstrous spill. When his arm drooped, a second arrow punctured his chest. Staggering backward as if he had slammed into a glass door, he stared dumbly at the pulsating arrow, hypnotized by the infinite delicacy of the feathers' spicules.

Providentially, a third arrow struck his backbone. The jolt spooked him downfield in a freakish beeline. Rattled by the unexpected move, the archers surrendered a dozen free yards with wild wing shots before they pin-cushioned the big man with a picture-perfect fusillade. He stumbled in a sinking pirouette, the slung hammers splaying like tassels.

Sprawled beneath a pitiless sun, he clawed off his mitt to finger the onetwothreefourfive braided cords of the hammers still looped over his shoulders. Scorched by memories of laughter erupting in the stands when a blinded, all-but-gone player lost yards and points to a dying burst in the wrong direction, he flailed to fix on some unmistakable landmark. *Downfield*! *Downfield*! he howled through a bloody slobber. And although he bowed to no God, his howl was a kind of prayer, a plea for guidance, or more precisely, *direction*. Streaked with paints of sweat and spit and blood fused with black clay-dust and white chalk, the big man clutched his hammers and heaved upward, splitting his wooden chest with a final wedge of air. Rising triumphantly to his knees, he began to earn inches.

Downfield.

\* \* \* \* \*

"Ooooo, there's the dinger," groaned the lounger watching the monitor. "That's that."

"No! He's up!"

"A sitting duck, kid."

"No! He's crawling. He might still—"

Thunder from the stands rumbled through the ceiling and rattled the lockers. The watching players dispersed. The newbie, left standing alone, burrowed into a litter of kibitzers clustered around the card table.

"That Polack just did ten hammers," he said in a hushed tone.

The fortyish woman scarfed up a discard. "Ten hammers isn't doable, pup."

"Ten."

"In your wet dreams maybe. Take it from a lady who's been waiting here since your Mama called you a case of indigestion."

"Sixty-four yards. Held all ten. It's a record."

"Wait for the points—" said the lounger, lifting his towel to smirk. Something in the newbie's face silenced him, however. The face appeared to shine like the haloed, overhead bulbs. It glowed with awe, pride, reverence, fear, jealousy, shame, and more – with every vital feeling that empowered the boy's thoughts; with every luminous thought that enlightened his feelings. The lounger recalled his own face, time out of mind, and lowered his towel.

"Hearts," grumbled the old-timer, flicking a red ten onto the discard pile.

"Who needs hearts?" griped his opponent, drawing from the deck.

The old man waited patiently. He cocked an ear when his opponent, lost in thought, muttered something.

"I can't hear you, Liz. What're you saying?"

"Nothing. Nothing, I'm just thinking."

"You can't think nothing."

"About the Polack, I guess. About ten hammers."

The old man gnawed his cigar. "Ten hammers is a Goddamm good bit all right."

The woman studied her cards.

"So whacha gonna do, Liz?" the old man said.

"You know Goddamm well I'm doing Babies, George. Why ask such a dumbass question? You saying I'm not a woman? You saying I'm—?"

"I'm saying where's your discard."

"Oh, *that*."

"Toss the ten," said a kibitzer.

The woman spat toward the bucket and glared. "Who the hell are you, sweetie, Edmond Hoyle? You want to play, grab a chair, and ante-the-fuck *up*."

The kibitzer blushed.

The woman shook her head and examined her cards. All in all, they were good cards. Some she had chosen, some she had drawn. All in all, about what she could expect – certainly no worse. Plenty to work with, lots of possibilities.

Eyes open, she pondered her play.

## 5.  A COMEDY OF MANNERS

Boot camp hootches were large, green-canvas tents anchored to a permanent, 2x4 frame. Hootches housed sixteen bunks – eight on either side of a center aisle. In my hootch, the *dramatis personae* included Wonder-bread whites, a Canadian, a couple of Mexicans, a Hopi Indian, and one splib dude – a wiry, little black guy from Oakland named Post.

Post had drawn the lead bunk just to the left of the front hatchway. First night – all of us busy stowing gear in green, wooden footlockers – Post said offhandedly, "Listen, guys, I know what's what, dig? We're stuck here together, can't be off to our own kind, and you're wondering how you can act, what you can say around me. So just know, I know what's what. People, they got to talk. Can't be watching every word. So if you was

to say something on accident, just know, I know
what's what."

The hootch fell silent until a tall, goofy-looking
kid volunteered a cautious, "You mean we could
like ... *slip* or something?"

I forget the goofy kid's name, but come to
recall, he was the Canadian. Drafted as a
"resident alien" or some such, he kept
bellyaching that he didn't have to stay, as if
staying were a favor to the rest of us. He washed
out about 4th week. Asthma, I think. Sucks to his
ass-mar!

Post – breaking in his new boots – was
squatting bare-chested beside his bunk. Without
looking up he said, "You mean if you slip and say
nigger?"

A few titters egged the goofy kid on. "Yeah.
That."

An overhead light illuminated the hatchway
like a stage. Post's sinewy, black back and chest
glistened with fine sweat. The goofy kid –
standing heaven knows why in white boxer
shorts atop his footlocker – was a gangly,
scarecrow form spotlighted directly opposite
Post, stage right.

"Slips are slips, man. Go ahead," Post said affably, raising his head. "Call me a chocolate nigger."

The audience saw Post's eyes and *immediately* became absorbed with belts and socks and brass. Myself, I was mesmerized by the play. The goofy kid – probably a little taken with his star turn – missed the cue.

"Okay," he chuckled through a shit-eating grin. "You're a chocolate nigger!"

Post exploded from the floor, his fist tracing a dark arc that landed smack in the goofy kid's toothy face. The kid tumbled across his bunk, crashed onto the plywood deck, banged his head on a hootch support, and started to cry.

"That one weren't no *slip*," said Post.

Next morning, critics panned Post's performance as over the top. I can't recall a one, however, who failed to find it compelling.

## 6. AIRBORNE

*If* it happened, it happened like this.

Mopping up after a firefight, a few pranksters commandeer a prisoner. Usually they pick a man – a sniper, maybe – but frankly, the joke is the thing, not the butt of the joke, so choice is no great weight.

They roughhouse the little, dark man or whatever to the dust-off and scramble aboard an urgently rocking chopper. The chopper shudders, cants forward, and is airborne.

Inside – hunkered together licking wounds – the stricken squad is numb, disinterested, silently beyond protest in a stayed-up-all-night, end-weary way. But the gadfly pranksters needle and prod like high school cutups goading listless seniors into some obligatory hoo-hah, some boozy, first-light panty raid.

"Watch," they shout over the noisy tattoo of the engine. "Watch!"

They tweak the little man's nose, flick his ears. They taunt him. In English, right? He doesn't understand English! And his own words – Pidgin phrases or Vietnamese – have all been spent. Eyes down, he kneels dumbly.

What fills his head besides the plangent, rolling thunder of the rotor blades? Anything, probably. Anything *else*. Perhaps he counts and recounts rivets in the cold, metal deck. Perhaps he summons memories of some lost brother, thoughts of roads taken and not taken. Or truer things, stories *without* words. The touch of warm bedclothes, early light through a window, the smell of breakfast, his mother's voice, the taste of tea – something good, if anything good is left.

The squad starts to snicker.

The little man doesn't know yet – which has to squeeze his heart – but then, when does anyone know?

Until one of the pranksters clangs open the hatch.

*Now* he knows. For *sure*.

*Now* he starts to jabber. WANNA WANNA WANNA GO'ING GO'ING GO'ING like Sid Caesar or Jerry Lewis doing their Chinese shtick. Man, the squad laughs at that. The wind-roar and flup-flup-flup of the rotor drown his words – all just silly jabber to them anyway – and who cares! *Words* don't matter. WANNA WANNA GO'ING GO'ING. The *sound* of the words is enough for the joke. The look on his face is enough – the clown-eyed, I-don't-fucking-believe-this look while his mouth flaps like a flag.

Never much ado. Out he goes. WANNA WANNA WANNA! Clawing at sleeves, but out no matter.

And then the part that gets the *big* laughs.

He tries to *fly*!

Men don't fly, but his arms beat the air. He flails and thrashes. Probably just instinct, that infant, falling instinct where the arms shoot up and clenched fingers try to grab hold mother. They say it *looks* like flying, though, and I've heard it's the same each time. No one ever stiffens or dives. No one looks resigned. They all try to fly.

*If* it happened, I would have shut my eyes. But, honestly, the laughter might have been irresistible. You see, I hadn't laughed at anything since before I was born and I agonized that I would *ever* laugh.

So if it happened, it might have been that the pranksters were dead-on. Because, face it! It's just too ludicrous, you know? Too fucking funny. That whole, Goddammed, frantic free-fall is so ridiculous an image, my laughter might have rung out with the rest of them, peeling like a school bell, all of us just *certain* that the little, dark man was laughing, too, when – WANNA WANNA GO'ING GO'ING – he hit, splat, against the earth like a newborn flopped onto his mother's tit.

## 7. COUNTING COUP

Stalled in the doldrums of something like sleep, Marlow basked in a strangely familiar sensation.

*First it was warm and then it was cold.*

Instantly he regretted summoning the words. Using ham-handed crayons of words to cartoon the razor immediacy of the warm then cold feeling was fool's work made tragic because the words *supplanted* the feeling. He felt the sensation waning like a betrayed and fading Tinkerbelle. He longed to renounce the words, but, already, they had conjured the image of a thin, green, paperback book. Marlow recalled the book, but not the words of the title. Struggling to remember the title played out additional lines of association whose drag, like a sea anchor, hauled him ever farther from the equatorial languor of sensation toward the colder clime of nominative consciousness.

The clamminess that he felt was his – he mouthed the words – bloody shirt. He hoped someone would come soon to change the shirt, but when no one came – forgetting to remember the book – he opened his eyes.

Marlow lay exposed, propped against a fan of thick stalks. Surrounding him, the steamy jungle was a murky, green, netherworld beneath a dark canopy. A sultry rain, filtered through the canopy, plopped erratically like large drops of condensation falling from a shower ceiling. Elephant ear leaves trapped the drops, sagged, spilled, then sprang up again, bobbing like toy birds around a glass. One enormous leaf – arched over Marlow like a green umbrella – dripped water from its scalloped edges. Extraordinarily thirsty, Marlow inched his back across the stalks until he felt a warm trickle against his supplicant tongue.

During moments of sleep or whatever, wavering columns of mist rising from the lush, jungle floor appeared as wraiths singing his

childhood counting song – the one-little, two-
little, three-little Indians song. The singing was
probably gunfire still ringing in his ears, but his
floundering mind seized the song like a tow line.
Pointing with his left hand – his slashed right
hand busy compressing a bayonet wound in his
belly – he began to count Indians.

One-little..two-little..three-little Indians, limbs
akimbo, lay touching – sprawled X's marking the
spot where a small enemy squad collided with
Marlow's four man patrol. The first little Indian,
a radioman, rested face up. Indians two and
three stretched face down. Within their intimate
triangle the radioman's dislodged helmet
collected raindrops like a bowl placed to catch a
leak.

Four-little..five-little..six-little Indians were
harder to spot, mingled with foliage like a
Hidden Pictures puzzle in his *Highlights for
Kids*. Number six was merely a foot protruding
from a bush. Marlow spied the foot only because
a dropped rifle, caught in a notch of crossed
stalks, called attention to the bush. A foot was
not necessarily a whole Indian, of course; Marlow
had seen the elephant and certainly knew *that*

much. He counted the foot nevertheless because the skirmish had been strictly rifles, cutting tools, fists, teeth – nothing that tore bodies apart and sent feet flying.

Seven-little..eight-little..nine-little Indians required no such judgment calls. When the firefight exploded, Marlow had whirled, spraying rounds promiscuously as if the countryside itself were attacking. The seventh little Indian – a black Lance Corporal from Jim Hogg County Texas – had ducked behind elephant ear leaves. Perhaps his terror-rattled reflexes had seized on the Cowboys'n' Indians rule that foliage stops bullets. *Those* games, however, were from another time. Hit by Marlow's wanton shots, the seventh little Indian had burst from the brush and fallen like a sparrow. The eighth little Indian – still clutching a bayonet – was a dead weight straddling Marlow's sleeping left leg. And the ninth little Indian – also propped against stalks – sat facing Marlow.

Although nine wore a different uniform with a black bandana instead of a helmet and had almond eyes in a dark face and was smaller than Marlow and altogether dead, which Marlow imagined himself not to be, it felt to Marlow as if he were gazing at a mirror. Unnerved, he looked away, searching anxiously for the tenth-little Indian to finish the Goddamm song.

One-little..two-little..three-little Indians, he began again, aloud this time, his left index finger wagging like a choirmaster's.

Four-little..five-little..six-little Indians.

Seven-little..eight-little..nine-little Indians.

Nine, Goddamn it! *Nine.*

He was fucked! Totally fucked, fucked for sure. He recounted, but fucked is fucked.

*Up and at 'em little cowboy*, said a voice in Marlow's head that sounded like his father rousting him from bed for school. Marlow hated school, but gritted his teeth and kicked free of the eighth little Indian as he would a tangled blanket. Goddamm if he would sit counting ten little Indians when the tenth was MI-fucking-A.

Bracing his open belly with his hand, lest the tender things inside spill out, Marlow poled to his feet against his empty rifle and stood wavering like the columns of mist he had heard singing. Heedless of direction, he began to walk. His firebase was several klicks to the east, but, just then, *every* direction in the netherworld was the same. All were *away*.

He couldn't shake the song, however, or the pictures stuck in his head of the little Indians. Marlow shouted, slapped his temple, counted steps and trees, even *leaves*! But the melody and pictures would not be dislodged. *Nine* Goddamm Indians was a forlorn hope, a story without an ending, an unfinished painting, a roundelay he could sing till doomsday.

And dying soon was not something Marlow felt he could count on.

## 8.  A FORE-EDGE PAINTING

*The Art of Forensic Science*

When finally I lost count and began to sob *too* much, a half-drunk Graves Registration Major spluttered a God-country-corps lecture and transferred me from incoming body bags to Forensics – a windowless, cinderblock box at the rear of our Da Nang complex where I could still *hear* the trucks and forklifts, but not see them unless I closed my eyes.

Assigned to unidentified remains, I invoiced bagged bits of bone and teeth, shards of skull, moldering corpses stumbled upon when some teeter-tottering map quadrant tipped again.

Human and inhuman debris were often commingled, however, since hasty soldiers confused pieces of men with animal bones, broken pottery, sticks, or what-have-you. Procedure specified that human matter be gleaned, inventoried, and whenever possible matched to correct service numbers.

It was a mad enterprise, mad like the Nazi compulsion to tattoo and issue death certificates to interchangeable Jews, madly bureaucratic in the way bureaucracies become insane at their compressed and rotted cores – not with the madness of storm, but of doldrums.

Nevertheless, I stopped sobbing. Forensics became an anodyne, as madness often does. Numbed with the transcendental remove of submersion in detail, I winnowed my bags, counted and re-counted the items within, noted their origin, nearby forces, and how the weather was.

When I had completed my invoice for the onetwothreefourth time and displayed the human remains in good light, a Forensic Specialist began his examination with telltale belongings, shreds of clothing, hair, tattoos, dental work. If such clues were insufficient, he stripped distracting flesh from certain pieces to expose hidden lines where sinew gripped bone. Measuring such lines and matching his measurements to arcane tables, the Specialist could make a man! Height, weight, sex, health, race, age ... on and on. Finding among profiles of the missing a match for his creation, the Specialist restored to the remains its number.

This conjuring of a man, so infinite in faculty, from bone to assign the bone a number was wondrous. Why, sometimes – sculpting features onto a fleshless skull – a Specialist summoned its face. Mostly the faces were indifferent as I imagined the dead to be, but occasionally – rigorous techniques employed *religiously* – a sculpted face would smile or frown or scowl or question. Had something *other* than sinew imprinted the bone? Had the specialist also summoned a trace of jest or fancy, a glimpse of soul?

While fascinating, such speculation impeded the methodical invoicing and gleaning of my bags. Hence, I found it necessary to remind myself from time to time that in the final count only numbers and bones remained. Or in a truly *ideal* world, bones correctly *numbered*.

### A Minor Cord

Body bags sometimes slipped off the peoplemovers since men are floppy and do not stack as well as, say, wood. This one guy – 1st MarDiv by his tattoo, crazy how you remember them – he flopped off the pallet and split the zipper of his green bag. Bloated and overripe, he burst a little when he hit, soiling my scrubbed and scrubbed and re-scrubbed deck with his greasy putrefaction. His face was all screwed up like it hurt or something, but that's *crap*. Believe me, dead men don't hurt. *At all.* They don't care when they fuck up your count and they don't clean their fucking mess. They sure don't fucking scream. Not even when they fall off the fucking forklift. That's never fucking *them* you hear screaming!

Using wide shovels, a trio of us hefted the fucker into a new bag and moved him along. But switching bags, I saw just how messed up he

was. Loose parts. Missing parts. Just too
jumbled, you know.

The mortuary PFCs fixed his ass anyway and
bounced him home. A job is a job, maybe, but
Goddamm! Some of those people were so trashed,
they should have gone home as ashes.

If at all.

### *Siren*

Saigon summer. Before the Fall.
Steamy streets.
Sweaty throngs shouting, shoving.
Foul puddles.
Bad air. Sour sweat and seared pork masking
the stink of Graves Registration. Embalming
fluid. On my hands, in my skin. Indelible. Like a
tattoo.

Mopping my brow. Hot skin, wet skin. Unlike
sapless skin in body bags, unlike clammy,
morgue skin. Blotting the palm on a sticky shirt.
Sweat trickling down where the shirt isn't stuck,
itchy runs like marching ants.

Summer streets. Simmering streets.

Too hot. Fever hot. Find a hole. *Any* hole.

Two deep at the sweltering bar. Wilted khaki collars. Soppy khaki armpits. One-two-three woof-woof ceiling fans, too high, too slow. Motion. Any motion. Arm motion. Two-shot whiskies, one-two-three.

One-two-three writhing stripper-girls sweating under color-wheel lights. Jiggling jello-mold breasts. Mounded mocha nipples. Sequins of sweat glistening red, yellow, blue. Silver, stripper panties peeled and discarded like one-two-three coruscating rinds. Peeled, dimpled asses grinding to The Doors.

Cigarette smoke coiling like mist over swamp. Eyes in the mist. Voodooed eyes, zombied and cinder-cold, beyond pain like morgue eyes, like eyes in body bags. Creature eyes in the mist, watching and watched. Eyes peeping. Eyes peering. Mouse-eyes, fox-eyes, owl-eyes. Eating and eaten eyes.

A woman's eyes, dark and glistening like black water in sooty torchlight. Not bedroom eyes. Not dead room eyes. Mired between here and there eyes. *Sick*room eyes. Eyes sick-heavy with a wet-congested fever stare like a hot, wet exhalation,

like a festering miasma rife with some base
contagion.

Worming up to the bar. Pressing a naked arm
against my arm, her flushed fever-flesh like my
flesh, unlike morgue flesh. Mouthing
*Marrr..lowww* from my name tag in a hot,
beckoning whisper, her breath fermented and
full, like spoiled cider, like bad air.

Gliding away, drawing me through the crush
in her sinuous wake. Past three dimpled asses,
past four rumbly speakers throbbing with The
Doors. Down one-two steps to a low, dark
passage, to one-two-three closed doors, to muffled
'*Fuck offs!*' growled at rattled latches. One-two
bodies, wordless, not touching. Two bodies full-
sick. Waiting for a door.

Gaunt body in a loose, yellow dress. Ligature
straps over haggard shoulders. Meager hips
cocked contrapposto. White, rawboned legs
stained with inkblot bruises. Pale, starveling tits
streaked with trickling sweat like marching ants.

An opening door. A small, dark whore
scurrying away. A khaki sergeant, fumbling at
his zipper, stumbling behind.

Barging into the puddled pisser, slamming home the bolt. Wheeling to pin her face-in-face against a broken mirror. Forcing my tongue between fevered lips. Spoiled-cider breath spilling like hot liquor.

A strident *NO!* Wrenching her head away, yanking her yellow dress over bare hips, balling the cotton into white belly-flesh like a rag staunching a wound.

Sinking to smell her, test her in a lizard way. Drowning my face in a tangled, black delta dammed between closed, white thighs.

Twisting aside, hoisting me, fingers like talons in my hair. Whirling to face the mirror. Arching her hips.

Grabbing her shoulders, spinning her toward me, worming into hot belly-flesh.

Pounding my chest, driving me back, tearing at my buckle, scratching my pants to the puddled floor. Hiking her dress. Turning, bracing, canting forward. Arching her naked hips with a cat's spastic urgency.

Falling into her through that other door, slathered and readied. Feeling her stiffen in rigor *vitae*. Thrusting. Counting thrusts. Clenching her waist. Squeezing air from her body. Filling the vacuum. Pulling out. Reeling back.

Cheek pressing the mirror, gasps fogging the glass. Wide eyes seeing nothing, probing tongue tasting nothing, open mouth receiving nothing. Rubbing, kneading, slapping and seized – a spasm like a stifled sneeze, one coiled, replete moment, her eyes rippling and subsiding like a dark pond disturbed from below.

Wiping with her hand. Smearing the wall. Rocking her hips to settle the dress. Throwing the door bolt. Gone!

Retreating.

To the bar. To whiskies, four-five-six. To the barracks. To the shower. To castigation of harsh soap and hot water. Hunkering sleepless in my rack, steeped till dawn in that miasma I had felt, that hot, wet, contagion recapitulated in cautiously squeaking springs.

Subsequent hot nights, if the woman acknowledged me at all, she grimaced as at something soiled, used, and utterly too familiar. Glued to my barstool, I watched her cull unsullied names to that subterranean passage, watched her emerge from the lower darkness like some exquisite mephitis, watched her wind through the crowd, her starving eyes fixed dead on the exit door.

And each time I saw her I felt a catch in my breath from that contagion, that miasma. Each time the memory of her wet, fermented whisper, her prolonged and puckered *Marrr..lowww* stirred a black sludge inside me, loosed the foul bubbling of a malignant need dark and disowned.

Why, even *now,* recalling her *right now,* I feel that catch, feel that stirring,, and once again I'm holding on, holding it in, suffering it, savoring it. I'm teetering at inevitability. I'm tottering above some singular resolution, I'm counting seconds, holding on. I'm counting minutes, holding my breath.

Holding.

Holding.

And I'm letting go.

Or die.

### *Magic Slate*

Remember magic slates? A clear plastic sheet over a milky film atop a black, waxy backboard. You drew on the slate using a red stylus that

slipped into a loop at the top of the thing, and
when you lost the stylus you just used your
fingernail to make lopsided houses, lollypop
trees, stick men, and faces.

Do they sell those anymore? I'd buy one if they
did. It felt good, that magic slate. The way your
nail slip-slid over the clear plastic coversheet
trailing a magical black line on the milky film.
The touch and especially the *sound* of lifting the
sheets to erase a picture not to your liking. The
way the milky film stuck to the waxy backboard,
resisting erasure with the persistence of memory!

Sometimes you lifted ever so slowly, one tiny
tug at a time, savoring the ripping dehiscence of
the film splitting free bit by bit. And other times?
A cavalier flick of the wrist, a crackly whisk, and
*abracadabra!*

A clean slate.

## 9. SNOW GLOBE

10 AUG 68

Guantanamo Bay

So, how do I describe Cuba *this* time, Marlow? The weather part, I mean. Mention the rest and you'd just accuse me of whining again, so that's that. But I have to say *something* if I'm going to keep writing, and at least the weather I don't bring on myself, now, do I?

The thing is, though, weather is as tough to talk about as anything else. People think they're saying something when they say it's hot. But what does it mean, hot? You told me once that Eskimos have like a hundred words just for snow, so maybe Eskimo-to-Eskimo they get the snow talk down pretty good. But what about sweaty-sheet nights or muggy, week-long afternoons when you're so Goddamm, sopping wet you just want it to rain and finish the job? An Eskimo wouldn't *comprendo*, because Cubans are upside down on the bottom of the world with a hundred weird words for hot. No, you don't know weather till you feel it, man, and even then you won't know what you don't know.

Tonight the hot is *aliento del Diablo,* breath of the devil. You collect words, man. Consider those a gift from your old, friend, Don. Take them in for share day some time, ha-ha.

Right now it's oh-dark-thirty and every dumbass in Cuba is wrestling sleep on sheets so sweaty they stick like Saran wrap. I'm burrowed in the head, myself, a cool cement hidey-hole all to my lonesome, just me in my skivvies hunkered in between rows of white sinks and shitters, all marble-cool like even rows of ... oh, I don't know ... snowmen, maybe. Sure, snowmen. Because that's what I'm thinking about. Snow. *Real* snow. Not that thin, white sheet pulled over the ground we called snow in Saginaw, but thick blankets of snow. Deep, white-powder comforters of snow.

Look, if you're wondering why I bother to keep writing with the weather report, it's because I figure that, one of these times, if you're still alive, you'll cut me a huss and shoot me back a fuck-off or something. Not just because I was wrecked when I wrote you that crazy letter, but because the shit I dumped on you wasn't the truth, even if it was true. You're a detail freak, so I'm betting you catch that little *hidden bunny* in the big picture one of these times. Meanwhile, even an empty envelope shows me you're getting my letters – that the gooks haven't bagged your ass. Otherwise, I'm in the dark, buddy, since who knows what happens to letters sent to dead Marines? Would they return them? Not likely. I mean, how would they stamp them?

Cancelled?

Discharged to God?

No, those letters probably rot in some dead-letter bin. And the point is, Marlow, I'd like to know you're still breathing, since neither of us much remembers the world without the other one in it. Every big thing we did, we did together, including the Green Suck here – up till this last part, where you're in 'Nam and I'm lying here waiting.

Actually I'm *not* anymore. Waiting, I mean. The point we thought we saw when we enlisted, what was it anyway? You had your Paul Revere thing going and, sure, that was cool, but a lot of it for both of us was simply getting out of school and being bored.

Whatever it was, it's gone now – eaten up by days policing butts on the parade deck and days swabbing heads and days spit-shining shoes and squaring away my socks just so and days polishing every fucking metal thing that is.

I mean … garrison duty? Who knew from *that*, man? Radio school was bad enough since you laid it out pretty plain when we started. One-two-three-go, right? Infantry, 'Nam, home as heroes, then on to the next thing. Still, radioman would have been good over there, in the jungle, in the boonies, kicking ass and taking names. But garrison duty? Garrison is—

Fuck it! I promised to stick with the weather. Well, tonight we have *aliento del Diablo*, buddy. A breath off the Caribbean stinking of bad fish; a hot, wet breath loaded with salt you can taste, salt like acid; salt that corrodes and rusts and crumbles *everything* unless it's scrubbed and cleaned and polished and scrubbed and cleaned and polished, and it all fucking rusts *anyway*. I can almost hear it right now – everything decaying with little creaks and cracks and groans. Everything falling apart.

But, like you said in *your* letter, I made my choice, so I need to stop whining. Exactly! Radio school was *my* choice. Believe me, man, I read you five by five.

So there you are.

And here I lay.

Only, who says you always like what you pick? Take that first liberty from Pendleton when we jumped on a Greyhound to Disneyland, off to find Annette, and you ended us up on that Small

World fucker that just never, ever, ended! You
don't have to like what you picked, Marlow. So
write back, Goddamm you! We're blood-brothers,
and I say that means you have to write back
regardless of anything. Scratch your arm and
mix the blood, you have to write back. Look it up.

What were we when we did that ... eight? One
more of your big ideas. Like everything else. Like
enlisting. All you, man.

So here I lay me down to sleep at Gitmo pretty
much played out by ditting and dahing and
scrubbing and folding and rotting from the devil's
breath. And what I'm wishing is that I had
something to read. That must sound strange
since you know I hate to read, but I really looked
forward to reading your letters, man. I always
expected to find the *next* big idea, like where we
go from here.

So I wish you would've kept that Goddamm
lecture in your last Goddamm letter to yourself,
buddy, Maybe just tell me the weather. But no,
you had to say how disappointed you are in me.
You had to rag on me getting wasted and my bad
choices. Like you *know*, man? Like you have
*words* for my choices?

Well, hot is not just hot and all the snow is different, motherfucker!

Here's a pop quiz for you. The day we met … August before first grade, a dripping hot day, sure to rain, remember? Mom was bitching out the movers, trying to cram a houseful of stuff into that stinkhole apartment she found near her sister after Dad died. It took me a long time to get over that; not the apartment – him dying. I *hated* him for it. I know that sounds mean, but I was only six, and maybe that's how it works until you're old enough to realize that dying is rarely a choice. And guess what? Lately I've even come to dig how he went.

Remember those black flies in Ontonagon? July is so thick with them you stay inside with every screened window open hoping to catch a breeze. Dad hollered for me to turn on the Tiger game and fetch him a Strohs'. He warned me to keep my eyes open because Kaline was ripe to sock one over the wall. He cranked back his Lazy-Boy and stretched out so the window fan blew over him. He was home, man, *really* home, all cool and comfy and content with no idea his number was up. No idea that something corroding inside him – something he didn't even know the word for – was fixing to break. And I see now how perfectly perfect it was. So cool and gentle. No noise, no fuss. Like a TV tube going bad maybe, and I bet he just faded away like the little dot does on the screen.

Anyway, I'm in Saginaw 'cause Mom's crying all the time and needs her family. She's busy, so I'm scoping out the new neighborhood for a friend and find you in your side yard hitting balls all alone. No one hits balls alone, man. *No* one. I'm thinking maybe you need a friend, too, and, sure enough, we start hitting together. You came off a little nuts, by the way – how you were counting up the flies and grounders and foul tips and whiffs in that goofy way you had of counting things. But I got used to it pretty quick, since it was just you, just your way. Most guys would remember those numbers, what they added up to, anyway – like which one of us was hitting long balls and which one was dribbling a grounder or two between whiffs. But *you* don't, do you? Because that *wasn't* your way. It was never about being 'better than' with you, Marlow, at least, I don't remember it so. Not once. So who could hate you, motherfucker, when better was just who you were? And who wouldn't want to scratch his arm and be a blood brother when all he really was, was some tagalong Tonto?

But here's the quiz, man. I'm wrecked, but I haven't forgotten the quiz.

What did you say to me that day? You won't remember, because you were too busy counting things that didn't count. What you said was, *let's try harder*. And here's what I didn't say back. Not then and not all the other times you couldn't count because you didn't know.

I *was* trying hard, man. As hard as I could.

I can almost hear you saying Cuba won't kill me. And, for sure, 'Nam is pure number ten. So I feel all wrong feeling this way again, but I do, so I'm saying it. You can't go schooling a blood brother about how he gets through each fucked day, because how do you know what it's like for him? He's got words you haven't heard, words you won't know till you walk in his moccasins – isn't that what they say? But here's the true skinny, buddy. You won't fucking know anyway, because the Tonto's moccasins won't fit you the way they do him, so keep your fucking judgments about me and my world to yourself, or fuck you twice, Keemosabe!

* * * * *

Sorry, man. I went off on you again, and I told myself I wasn't going to do that. But, I'm cool now. It's later, real, *real* late, and I'm cool again. Maybe we'll both finish this if I stay cool and stick to the weather report, just go with the flow like we did up in Ontonagon that summer, floating downriver on those black inner-tubes toward that big-as-an-ocean lake, drifting along all cool and lazy talking about nothing – how hot it was and the chance it might rain, and underneath it all thinking about snow, because when everything is one way, you can't help but think of another.

Hot and snow. They go together, see? Maybe that's why I was so hung up on that snow globe I brought back from R and R in Miami. I never told you about the Goddamm thing, so picture it. Me in Cuba toting around a snow globe like a pacifier. Sometimes I pestered Post with it.

Remember Post? The splib dude from boot camp? He wound up here, too, so maybe it *is* a small world after all, ha-ha!

Anyway, I used to bug Post about the little house inside the snow globe, telling him it was where I was born. He always rolled his eyes with a "Shee-it, man! Ain't no real house *ever* looked so whitebread as that snow globe house."

I think he was saying something about the house's phony shutters, too crooked walkway, snow covered pines, and the way light seemed to ooze through the frosted windows like syrup. Maybe that's whitebread to Post, but, really, what does he know? Not what he doesn't know, that's for sure. And what he doesn't know is a hungry hole stuffing itself with what he *does* know – Oakland. But the world isn't Oakland, just like it isn't Saginaw or Cuba or 'Nam or even Ontonagon. Sure, the two houses *looked* different, but the truth is, minus details, that snow-globe house was an honest-to-God twin of the one I moved from, the one up in Ontonagon where my Dad died watching a Tiger game, the one I used to pretend I still lived in.

For a while down here, I was brooding a lot about home, knowing, deep inside, it was as long gone as that pretend house. I spent days fretting about it – moping and shaking my snow globe, watching the snow swirl and settle over everything.

Bad luck for me, though. A glass thing lives on borrowed time in this hard-rock world, and one particularly harsh night my snow globe cracked. It was just a tiny crack at first, not even a leak, and Post couldn't dig why I was so blown away. But you're smarter than Post and me put together, so maybe you can see how a cracked snow globe is at war with itself. Uncracked, the glass is invisible, so the house inside rises from nothing as it should. But cracked? The crack is like – oh, I don't know, a scar in your eye, maybe, like one of those white pupils blind guys have in movies, which is just more bullshit, of course, because when have you *ever* seen a white pupil? But if you *did* have a white pupil, and you weren't totally blind, I figure your eye wouldn't *just* see what it's seeing, but it would see itself, too. See the white scar. The *crack*. That tiny crack in my snow globe made my little house *part* of the globe, so the house itself was lost.

Finally, the globe broke completely. Without it I couldn't sleep at all, not during nights of *aliento del Diablo*. So Post – we're blood brothers now, too – he showed me a trick to make snow in my head. Oakland, he says, is like a desert, and head snow is about all you'll ever see there.

Well, damned if the house I discovered in my head wasn't truer than the snow globe house or the real house or the pretend house – truer even than *memories* of the pretend house, because – since nothing in the world made it look this way or that – the simple truth of shutter and pine and walkway and light was as pure as snow itself. I mean, it was number *one*, that house. No, even *better!* Like … *zero*, man! Because it was perfect, maybe *too* perfect, if that's possible, because how could you look away? Why mark time with anything less than perfectly perfect.

I don't think I can ever describe that house to you, though. My words would piss us both off. They'd be like cracks – you'd see the words, not the house, or maybe the words *and* the house, but not the house. So, maybe a good snow globe still has a place from time to time.

Stay cool,

Your friend, Don

*(UNOPENED)*

## 10. SMALL WORLD

Perched alone in the stern of a crowded boat sat a young man. The boat crept along a still, dark stream. The stream wound between tiered displays of smiley-faced dolls wearing cheerful, native costumes from various countries.

*No ... from **all** the countries. From every stinking country on the whole Goddamm planet,* fumed the young man. *Christ Almighty! How many countries can there be?*

He tried to remember the number, but couldn't concentrate over the background music – a broken-record chorus of children braying some lame-ass jingle about all the countries being one smiley-faced, little world. The number of countries was surely an answer he memorized in high school, since school was one, long funeral parade of useless numbers. 1066 and 38th parallel and Uranium 235 ... on and on! Not to mention the numbery things he couldn't get his head around at all, like why multiplying by zero was A-okay while dividing by zero was some mortal sin. But right when a number from high school might finally count, when knowing the number of countries might keep him from going ape-shit – Pfffft!

So much for high school and *all* its answers.

*Okay, ballpark it,* he thought, squirming like a scorpion doused with whiskey. *What's the worst case?* **Thirty** *countries? He could handle thirty.*

The squirming man flashed on a black-and-white TV image – Khrushchev pitching a bitch at the UN, a fat, old baldy pounding his shoe against a long, curved desk. He saw tiers of curved desks rising like bleachers, tiers of Jack Webb faced ambassadors sitting behind signs naming their countries. Name after strange name. Tier after tier, running off  the screen.

*Too many names.*

*Way too many countries!*

"This is screwed!" he blurted, shooting to his feet.

"Park it, you jamook!" growled a meaty man wearing a floppy, souvenir hat. A jester's hat.

"That song. It's eating my brain!"

"Sit *down*."

"I can't. My ass is on fire!"

"Hey! Watch the mouth. I got a lady here."

"Oh, Sal! Just ignore him," said the man's wife. "You're missing the Cuban dolls. Look, a burro. How sweet."

Sal swiveled, jingling the bells dangling from his jester's hat "Didn't we just see Cuba? Back there. I'm sure we did."

"No. I don't *think* so."

"Cuba doesn't *have* burros, Doris."

"That's a burro, you big silly!"

The standing man felt no air against his face, no sense of progress. Fixing on one doll, he seemed to be moving, but closing his eyes, he stalled.

"I can't take this anymore!" he moaned.

"Sit with me," offered a wispy girl in a yellow dress, scooting sideways. "It's more fun when you share things."

Glowing like television screens, the girl's glasses reflected the lighted dolls, the happy, humming passengers, and the standing man himself, hovering like an angry ghost.

"You, there! Standing. No standing!" barked a young man stationed in a bow seat facing backwards. He wore a visor cap with a badge. "Don't you see you're rocking the boat?"

Ripples, circling the boat like rings on a target, marred the water's glassy perfection,

"Are you in charge?" asked the standing man.

"No. I'm the conductor."

"Close enough. I want to go back."

"You can't. Sit down."

"No *really, I*—"

"Sit down."

"Oh, Sal, look! A burro!"

Sal's hat jingled. "Didn't we just see a burro?"

"No, I don't think so."

"You're not hearing me," the standing man pleaded, pushing forward. "I have to go back. Really! I *have* to go back." Lurching along the deck, he elbowed Sal's hat into the stream.

"You better shit me a new hat!"

"Hey! What happened to watch the mouth?"

The standing man stooped to fish the floppy hat from the black water. He gave it a jingly-jangly shake and plopped it back on Sal's bald head. "Good as new, see? I'll just scootch past you here so I can—"

"My toe! My toe!" yelped Sal, recoiling. The tiny boat yawed. The scootching man stumbled into Doris.

"He's copping a feel!" she squealed, clutching his hand tightly against her breast. "Sal, he's copping a feel!"

Yanking his hand free, the stumbling man knocked Sal's hat back into the water.

"What's your Goddamm malfunction, kid?"

The escaping man scrambled to the bow.

"Satisfied?" scowled the conductor. "It's ruined now. You've ruined the ride for the others."

"I didn't *mean* to!" the standing man groaned. "But I ... I can't do this anymore."

"Sir, your ride is in progress."

"Where's the proof of *that!* Look, I need you to—"

"Impossible."

"Hear me out! ... Okay, okay, I've decided. I've decided to wait for SpaceWars after all. Or ... or maybe Pirates of the Main. I had—"

"Hey! Big shot with the badge," barked Sal, wringing out his jingling hat. "Your little fanook's Daddy wasn't a glassmaker. Find him a seat or I will."

The conductor slid toward the railing and patted the bench. The standing man wedged himself into the bow seat.

"I had an E-ticket, see? An *E-ticket.*"

"And you got an E-ride."

"Well, it's a *fucked* E-ride."

"Tell me about it," grumbled the conductor. Removing his cap, he withdraw a pack of smokes hidden in the crown. He shook one out for himself and offered one to the sitting man.

"Sure, thanks, but ... can we smoke here?"

"No way! Place is a tinderbox," said the conductor, striking a match. "But I'm sporting the hat, right?" He lit his cigarette, inhaled, and grinned like a man scratching a jock itch. Smoke escaped leisurely through his nose. "God! ... Did I need *that*, or what!"

Refusing a light, the sitting man parked his cigarette behind his ear. "Tell me something," he said. "You seem normal enough. How can you stomach this?"

"Oh ... it's not so bad. I get to sit in front, wear the badge. Looking backwards is good, too, because I don't dwell on what's coming. Plus, I keep busy checking things off in my route-book. If you ask me, you should count your blessings."

"I didn't ask."

The conductor stubbed out his cigarette on the deck.

"All things considered, this ride is *cherry*, man. Picture the goofs stuck with Merry-Go-Round or that godawful Peoplemover."

"Don't lump me in with that A-ticket trash!"

"Count yourself lucky, my friend."

"LUCKY HELL!"

"Sal! Make that man be quiet."

Still massaging his toe, Sal glared. "You don't pipe down, kid, I'm gonna pound your ass like a taiko drum."

"I want SpaceWars," whispered the sitting man to the conductor.

"I'm afraid you made your choice."

"But I didn't *know*!"

The conductor swept his arm. "You knew as much as they did."

"Okay, look, here's the deal. I'll go back, see, but this time I'll do SpaceWars. No, wait, wait! ... Pirates of the Main."

The conductor pulled stubs from his pocket. "Your ticket ... it's been punched, see?"

"I'll explain. I'll get a refund."

"No refunds. It's printed plainly—"

"I *said* I'll go back!"

"You can't."

"Yeah? Try to stop me."

"Me? I couldn't stop you."

"Then I'll go back."

"You can't."

"But *why*?"

The conductor shrugged. "Because you *can't*."

The sitting man sprang from the seat and shoved his way astern. Halting at the rail, he looked backward. The black stream seemed deep and unbearably cold. The doll displays inched closer and closer together until they squeezed shut. A faint, V-shaped wake pointed forward like a one-way-street sign.

Crowding back into the bow, the standing man strained to see ahead. Dolls. More dolls. *Only* dolls. He sank back onto the conductor's bench, slumped forward, and shut his eyes. In darkness, all movement ceased. Ages slipped by ... or seconds, who could know? Suddenly the motionless man bolted upright, almost spilling from the teetering boat.

"I was humming! Did you hear it? I was humming the Goddamm song! I have to get off. Now! I have to go back. Right now! I have to—"

"Shhh!" hissed the Conductor. "Shhhhhhhhh!"

The standing man grabbed the Conductor's shirtfront. "I don't want to make a scene."

Sprawled across the first seat, a wiry, black man snickered. The standing man whirled.

"You got a problem, bro?"

"Got a solution ... *bro*. Dude's blowing smoke up your ass. You can switch rides."

The standing man tightened his grip on the conductor's shirt. "Give it to me straight this time."

"Well ... uh, *technically*, I guess, but—"

"SpaceWars!" whooped the standing man. "No, wait, wait. Pirates. Yes, Pirates!"

"No one gets it all," the black man drawled. "I never said a good ride, just a *different* ride."

"What the hell? Which ride?"

"Don't listen to him!" warned the conductor. "It's completely unauthorized."

The black man leaned forward and whispered, "Foggy Froggy's Blotto Bobsled. Whisks you straight to Peoplemover."

"PEOPLEMOVER! After sitting through this—"

"Shhhhhh. Shhh. Lower your voice," hissed the conductor."

"Look, Sal. A burro."

"Didn't we just see a burro?"

The standing man groaned. "*Please* tell me we're done with Cuba. Give me *that* much."

The conductor consulted a thick route-book covered with tick marks. "No ... Cuba, see?"

"Go for the Bobsled," goaded the black man. "Cool and quick."

"Not that Peoplemover part," snapped the conductor.

"You two aren't *helping*," the standing man said, sinking back into the bow seat.

The conductor dropped an arm over the sitting man's shoulders. "When life hands you dilemmas, make dilemma-nade, my friend."

The sitting man looked up. "You're an idiot, aren't you?" he said.

Unexpectedly some peripheral shadow, new or unnoticed, caught the sitting man's eye. "Wait a minute. What's that?" he said. "Over there."

"It's, uh ... nothing. Nothing at all."

"It's a door! Look, another one."

"You're not supposed to see them," the conductor said sheepishly.

"Where do they go?"

"Well ... nowhere, really."

"C'mon! Doors lead *somewhere*."

"They're short-cuts, that's all."

"Short-cuts to where?"

"To where the rides end."

"*All* of them?"

"Sure. Small World, SpaceWars, Merry-go-round, Pirates of the Main, Foggy Froggy, that godawful Peoplemover. All of them."

"Then what?"

"Then nothing. Ride's over."

"Look, Sal, a—"

"I know, Doris, I know, I know."

The unhappy man shook his head. "This is it, isn't it?"

The conductor shrugged. "What you see is what you get."

"But I mean *all* of it. All the way. It's all the same, right?"

"You made your choice."

"Gee! Thanks for keeping the tally straight, Mister-fucking-Obvious! Like I *missed* that part before? ... Okay, so answer me this. How many countries are we looking at?"

"Who could count!" the conductor sang out. "After Cuba we have the whole Caribbean. Then Africa. Then Micronesia, Polynesia, Melanesia, island paradise by island paradise. Australia, Asia and Europe. Then North America. Good God, can you *imagine* how long it takes to get through Canada? Then the States, zip code by zip code. Mexico. Central America. South America, degree by degree, from Ecuador through Tierra del Fuego and right on across the Drake Passage to ... Say!" he said. "We can sit here together. We'll only look backwards. We'll smoke and talk. We'll laugh if anyone grumbles. Put *that* in your hat, Sal!" he added sharply.

"So you're saying it's a *long* ride?"

Turning to glance ahead, the conductor froze momentarily. His eyes seemed to swell like sponges absorbing too much. With a shudder he buried his face in his route book and began to make tick marks.

"A *very* long ride, right?"

The conductor stopped counting. He looked up.

"It's an E-ticket, my friend."

The unhappy man felt as if images of dolls were etched onto his eyeballs, as if chirping children were recorded on his eardrums. The imprinted, seemingly fixed *now* obscured a myriad of choices, of new chapters in his one and only book – the satisfying cigarette tucked behind his ear, the beckoning seat beside the wispy girl, the easy friendship of the conductor, the comical testosterone of Sal the henpecked he-man, the jiggly bounty of Doris' breasts, the here-be-tigers world behind the wiry, black man's smirk. He was oblivious to wide-eyed children giggling and pointing; lonely people stealing glances; young sweethearts leaning together; old couples holding pale, veined hands. Dolls and the song were everything, now and forever.

Dolls and the song.

Dolls and the song.

Dolls and the song.

The unhappy man could not imagine another moment, another time.

He dipped his hand into the icy water and raised it to the light. His wet, dangling fingers sparkled like icicles. Crystal beads formed at the fingertips. The beads swelled, ripened, let go, and returned to the stream.

"Every door is the same, right?"

"All the same. Short cuts."

"I'll get off here then."

"Are ... are you *sure*?"

"If I don't have to hear this Goddamm song, I'm sure, I'm sure."

The boat approached a narrow, unlighted landing and door. The standing man stepped off.

"Good riddance!" muttered Sal.

The black man leaned back, closed his eyes, and smiled.

The conductor extended his hand. "It's not too late. Quick. Jump back aboard."

The standing man shook his head.

"Then ... then take these!" urged the conductor, fumbling for his cigarettes.

"Keep them. You got a long way to go."

The conductor tucked the cigarettes back into his cap, squared the cap on his head, and gave a wistful, two-finger salute. He opened his route book and licked his pencil.

"Stay cool," said the waiting man, but the boat had already slipped away.

So.

The waiting man plucked the cigarette from behind his ear and stuck it between his lips. He patted his pockets for matches, found none, and flicked the cigarette into the stream. It lay bobbing in the dark water.

So.

Ducking through the small door, the exiting man plunged into a deliciously warm darkness made perfectly black and silent when the door locked shut behind him. Pressing on, however, he felt as if he were passing too quickly from summer through fall to a cold, dark winter. Noticing tingles like tiny flakes brushing his skin, he fancied snow falling and began to shiver. The cold soon numbed him, however, like an injection of pain-killer. He *thought* he still walked, but his frozen feet made no sound, as if they were wading through feathery, dry snow rising over his ankles, his calves, his knees. He imagined himself crossing a vast, frigid, ever-dark continent, but – deaf, numb and blind – he might have been anywhere, which put him nowhere, so he halted, or *thought* that he did. For the first time in his life, he was still.

"S.Sal?" whispered a woman's voice.

"Shhhh! Ride's over."

The nowhere man thought about untold pirate ships, rocket cars, painted horses, Peoplemovers, and tiny boats, all gathered motionless in the dark, all vanishing beneath the implacable snow.

He thought he heard a muffled jingle and a faint, "Doris?"

"Shh! Ride's over. Shhhhh … shhhhhhh … shhhhhhhhhhh."

He thought he felt the insubstantial snow bury him; that is, he thought he felt nothing at all. And finally, *thinking* nothing at all, there was something like sleep

## 11. SHADOW RAY

Two loud-mouthed brothers lingered in the bar after last call, sulky Copper Harbor miners bemoaning a luckless fishing trip. I knew they were trouble. People who drink till closing generally can't help themselves. A live thing squirms inside them, like the worm inside a jumping bean, and sometimes – soaking so long in alcohol like a seed in water – the shell you *see* splits open freeing the live thing. Usually that's bad.

The shorter brother glared at Shadow Ray, the black porter mopping the floor.

"What you lookin' at, you one-eyed monkey?"

Shadow Ray had an empty eye socket – a sight so ugly, people cringed. Glass eyes are expensive and Ray was poor; but then, he didn't wear a patch either. I gathered that Ray lost the eye in a brawl that also crippled his left leg. Fifty-five or so, he hobbled like a hundred year old man.

"I *said* what you lookin' at?"

"Lookin' at a fool," said Shadow Ray, raising the mop to port arms.

Both brothers stood. I grabbed the taped billy club from under the register and vaulted the bar. Big brother blocked my way.

"Ain't your business," he snapped.

"*Is* my business," I said, slapping the club against my palm. "This man has work to do. Pay up and go home."

The short one spit on the floor. Like many miners, he had brown teeth, a legacy of unfloridated water and mean food.

"You some nigger-lover?" he said.

Shadow Ray tightened his grip on the mop handle.

"Damned if he ain't, Bobbie," said big brother, shoving me backwards. "I got me half a mind to—"

Words or no words, it was ending one way, so I whacked the club into big brother's left elbow hard enough to clip his wing. He howled like a ghost, hop-stepping and hugging his arm.

When the little one whirled, Shadow Ray bayoneted him up under the ribs with the mop handle. He folded like a jackknife and that was that, unless one of them pulled a gun.

"$19.50," I said, counting the dead soldiers on the table."

Left arm crooked against his side, big brother scratched right-hand awkwardly at an overall pocket for his billfold. It fumbled onto the floor, opening like a dropped book to a frequented page. A photo window – the clear plastic hazed with age like old people's eyes – held a snapshot of the brothers, two waifish, young wives, and a half-dozen brown-toothed kids.

"Give'm his money, Bobbie. Let's get the hell on home."

Still doubled over, little brother scooped up the wallet. He uncurled slowly, standing canted like a straggling runner with a side stitch. He clawed a twenty from the billfold, wadded it in his fist, and let it roll off his palm onto the floor. I picked up the bill, tailed the brothers as they nursed each other to the door, and flipped the latch behind them.

Shadow Ray returned to his bucket. I closed out the till and readied things for the morning man. Neither of us spoke.

When Hanson first hired Ray, I had welcomed
a helper. Within a week, I was ready to go it
alone again. Working together, it was hard to
keep your distance, and Ray was like a
porcupine. Get close, get pricked.

Finishing his chores, he pulled on a coat, but
stood fiddling with the buttons as if stalling to
say something. I wasn't betting on *thanks* or
even *good night* since I hadn't heard those words
in three whole months.

When Shadow Ray *did* talk, you knew he was
Southern, but details were sparse. I assumed he
was one of those men who come to a place, stay
for a while, and vanish. I knew he arrived on a
bus, same as I did, and that *his* bus came from
Chicago. More than that was imagination, but I
imagined he got off the bus when he found
himself about as far from a big city as he could
get going north around the Great Lakes.

Re-buttoning his last button, Ray started to
leave, but stopped at the register where I was
wrapping loose coins. Wordlessly, he tapped a
boot toe against the bar rail. Finally he said,
"Weren't no cause to take care of that, Mis-tuh
Marlow."

As a reminder that we were not friends, Ray called me 'Mis-tuh' with a sullen drawl that made it 'Mas-tuh' – less a black thing, though, than a one-size-fits-all anger at everybody. You saw the anger burning in his good eye and the cold ash of the burning in the icy hollow of the dead eye.

"Didn't want the bucket spilled, Shadow Ray."

"Shee-it," he said, plumping onto a stool.

Having learned early on that talking to Ray caused more problems than it solved, I kept my mouth shut. Finishing with the change, I stuffed the day's receipts and a deposit slip into a canvas money bag to carry to the night depository. Ray sat tapping his fingertips against the bar like a telegrapher pecking at his key. When the tapping stopped, he spoke.

"Know why I lost this eye?" he said, training the empty socket on me like the hole of a gun barrel.

"A fight."

"I asked *why*."

"No clue, Ray. You want to tell me?"

He looked at the mirror, aiming the empty socket at himself. After a moment he turned back.

"You know Little Rock?"

"Sure. I was there once."

"Shee-it, man ... you know *of* Little Rock. And nothin' at all 'bout where I growed up."

"Who could say, Shadow Ray? You've haven't *said* where you grew up?"

"I'm saying *now*. Growed up in colored-town, Mis-tuh Marlow. And that's a place the likes of you don't *never* know."

He paused, rubbing at something in his good eye. He blinked a few times, then added, "But my Daddy, he said, I could do better. Said school was how, and he whupped me good, ever time I hookied. Come time they reopen the high schools after them troubles, Daddy said I was finna go to Central where them soldiers done been. I wanted me no part of it, but Daddy said I'm better learned at the white school, and I knowed not to sass."

"First day, place looked plum peaceful. No mobs. No soldiers. A colored boy could walk right on in the school door like it was right."

"But inside? ... Shee-it, Mis-tuh Marlow, 'twas more than the eye-ballin' and the finger-pointin'. More than the mean tricks and the ugly things hung to my locker. Was the schoolhouse itself! All that aggravation done charged it up like some big ol' *hate* battery. Even off to yourself, you be tinglin' with stored up hatred runnin' through you. Get a crawly feelin' like when lightnin's 'bout to strike."

"One white boy, Tommy Ray, I knowed good. His Daddy owned him three Cities Service fillin' stations. Was my Daddy's bossman. And since Tommy Ray's Daddy preached 'bout the *new* south and such, Tommy Ray and me played together when we was little."

"Two Rays ... Ray and Tommy Ray. For a time, I stuck like a tick to that boy, so as folks in to callin' me *Shadow* Ray. World was a patch of woods and a junk yard 'round back the station. Stripped ol' cars, seats with sprung springs pokin' through, windshields all spider-web cracked. Lot of magic in a place like that, Mis-tuh Marlow."

"Me and Tommy Ray would eat us some of my mama's spoon bread and his mama's butter beans. Sometimes we'd chuck rocks at the dirt daubers. Sometimes we'd wade in the crick with Mason jars catchin' pollywogs, none of which ever growed to a frog, but just died in the jar. We tried to feed 'em – eggs, leaves – and was prob'ly the wrong food, but was also like them pollywogs died of spite. *Wouldn't* eat. Lonely for the pond, they was, and angry they was stole away – ain't about to take handouts from them what done it."

"Sometimes me and Tommy Ray snuck cigarettes. We'd lay 'cross them busted car seats and watch clouds and say what they might be and blow our own smoke-ring clouds that faded so purdy."

"But weren't like we was friends nor such. There was a line and you knowed – time come – everbody jump to they own side. Weren't no profit calling no white boy friend."

"But the year I come to Central, Tommy Ray, he tried to *act* my friend. Say 'hey' in the hall. Sit near me in class. He fetched some aggravation for it, but he was a pop'lar boy – had him a good family, money, a nice house – so most folks tolerated his antics, figurin' he meant no harm, that he was just tryin' to live the Good Book and too young to know what's what."

"'Round Thanksgiving – Tommy Ray's folks be off somewhere – he sneaked him a party to his house and said I could come. Just weren't done, Mis-tuh Marlow. Not then, not there. Oh, the schooled folks said 'colored' and 'Nigra' or even 'Nee-Gro.' And like Tommy Ray's Daddy, they went on 'bout everbody bein' the same. But weren't nobody who sat down together in they own house. *Nobody*."

"And thing was, it vexed me – him askin' me, him feelin' so *proud* 'bout askin' me, him not askin' me before. Shee-it, I said yes to plague him."

"Our houses was a *long* walk between, so that night, Tommy Ray come round to fetch me in his car. Man, that was one *good ol'* car, a shiny black Chevrolet used to be his Daddy's, a car *my* Daddy kept hummin' right on through the war, scarin' up tires and belts when ain't much to be had. Tommy Ray, he say he aimed to carry me home, too, maybe save me a whuppin', since, I was sure enough finna rile folks."

"Why in hell you doin' all this, Tommy Ray?"

"'Cuz you're my friend, Ray,' he said. Said it right out like that, Mis-tuh Marlow. Said it drivin' that sweet Chevrolet I ain't never rode to that fancy house I ain't never seen inside. 'And if I can't be friends to them what suits me – if I can't have 'bout *anybody* to my own house, then, Shadow Ray, I'm as much in chains as you.'"

"'Tommy Ray,' I said. 'You don't know the first *damn* thing 'bout chains.'"

"So he said, 'Look, you don't have to be no friend, you don't want, but irregardless, you my guest. Someone offend you, they offendin' *me*. I'll take care of it, you hear?'"

"Take care of it? ... Jus' 'cause his li'bral Daddy was rich, Tommy Ray reckoned he could *change* Little Rock. Shee-it! Ain't no changin' the core of things, man!"

"I go inside with Tommy Ray, folks was shocked. A hush come down like darkness hushin' the twilight chirpin' of the birds. Course, might've been that nobody spoke direct. Southern folks is mannerly. You in a man's house, rules say you respect the house. Payback, it can come another place, another time. Only the new South had new rules, so three older boys come over and say, 'You got to go, Shadow Ray.'"

"I told them boys I ain't got to do nothin' but die, and they said to suit myself, 'cause I'd be neither the first nor last."

"Tommy Ray said, 'You boys best behave! Shadow Ray is my friend and a guest to my house.'"

"The biggest of the boys, he had him a good upbringin' so he 'pologized for makin' a commotion. 'Folks know it's none your fault that your Daddy done twisted your head all round, Tommy Ray. But this here ain't the way things meant to be,' he said."

"I knowed weren't no profit in the situation and had me half a mind to go on and get my whuppin'. But Tommy Ray's words – 'I'll take care of it' – they come back bitter on me like bacon, and 'stead of leavin' I stood starin' at him like I was waitin' for an answer to a question."

"So scared his voice cracked, Tommy Ray told them three boys, 'I'll appreciate y'all to leave my house, else I call my Daddy.'"

"The biggest boy said, 'We'll respect you 'bout your house, Tommy Ray, but Shadow Ray, he goin' too.'"

"Tommy Ray hesitated, as that boy was sure enough drawin' a line."

"'You ain't near man enough to whup the three of us, Tommy Ray,' another boy said. 'And he ain't worth no ass-whuppin'. Not no nigger.'"

"There it was. Tommy Ray's eyes found mine. His face gloomed up, like when you think 'bout something you lost. He gave a little shrug, stepped 'twixt them boys and me, and shoved the big one toward the door."

"Tommy Ray, now, he was a strong ol' boy, but weren't no carouser. Pretty much kept to books and such. And that big boy, he weren't so easy to move. He hit Tommy Ray *hard*, bustin' his nose wide-open bloody. Tommy Ray's legs went rubbery and – lookin' confused – he dropped straight down to his knees. Big one grabbed him a fistful of hair and yanked Tommy Ray's head back."

"'Let it be, Tommy Ray,' he shouted 'Just let it be!'"

"That big boy let go the hair, and Tommy Ray – all wobbly like – poled to his feet and hit him square in the face, rockin' him back 'gainst the wall. People, they start to holler. Things was happenin' fast. All three boys jumped on Tommy Ray and was beatin' him right good. He looked to me, a plea in his eyes, and I heard myself shout top of my lungs, 'Go on Tommy Ray. Take care of it. Take care of me, high and mighty. Do it. *Do it!*'"

"If'n he heard me or not, I don't know. They was scufflin' pretty hard. And then, everwho come prepared, pulled a hammer from out his coat. There was a thud like you done pound your fist square on the butt of your palm. Tommy Ray, he stiffed up like starched pants. His arms shot down to his sides and his hands drawed back. His eyes rolled so just the whites showed and he fell like a tree."

"Most folks run. Some stayed to see. Tommy Ray's head gushed blood and he weren't movin' none. Them three boys, they looked horrified. Biggest boy said, 'See what you done? See what trouble you brung to this house! We finna whup you good.'"

"They lit in on me, three to one, and though I was big and been scrappin' all my life, it weren't enough. A firecracker went off right here inside my eye socket, a yellow ka-boom and I don't remember no more, 'cept, when I waked up in the hospital, that hammer done took this eye and a lick of my brains. Tommy Ray, he was dead."

A sad look came over Shadow Ray's face. He began to tap the bar again. No words, just a tap, tap-tap, tap. I waited.

"The town was right pained 'bout Tommy Ray, Mis-tuh Marlow," he said finally. "Still ... it was a ugly thing that most folks druther forget. But bein' as Tommy Ray's Daddy was rich, town up and *tried* them white boys. Two, that is. The big one's father was equal rich – family with the mayor and such – and that big boy, he swore Tommy Ray swung first; swore Tommy Ray knocked him stone-cold so he had no part in the fightin'. In the courtroom, he wore him a mess of bandages over his head and nose. Looked plum pitiful.

"Other two boys, they was from trash and had to answer. Not for cripplin' a black boy or takin' his eye. That was just fightin', they said. Boys was tried for manslaughter.

"Ones who spoke out, they told different tales. Ain't no one said plain who hit Tommy Ray with that hammer. And no one much cared what I said, since my memory weren't no good for a while. Turned out, though, they stuck them two boys in prison. One of 'em, I heard later, was abused pretty good and hung himself in his cell. Other one did his time and, best to my knowledge, never come back to Little Rock. I doubt prison made him any less mean, though. Could be, he's in another prison. Maybe he killed again or maybe he done got killed himself. And if'n he stayed clean and made him a family somewhere? Why, that's just 'nother bunch of boys raised to meanness. It's the way of things," Shadow Ray said.

"The rich one? I seen him ever now and then before I left town. His Daddy owned the hardware store and that boy, he always behind the counter if I needed me some nails. Or maybe a hammer.

"His Daddy died, that boy took the store and made out right good. Had him three children.

Sent 'em to the Baptist School. Last I heard, years ago, he was mayor himself.

"School said I was too ugly and crippled to go back, but seein' as Tommy Ray's Daddy was li- bral and bore me no grudge, he let me help out 'round the fillin' station 'til I was healed enough to git gone of Little Rock.

"But here's the thing, Mis-tuh Marlow … here's the thing. Me and Tommy Ray together, the *two* of us? We'd a-licked them boys. I *know* it. Alone, though? Three-to-one? That's easy pickin's. What chance got a boy alone? Yet *together?* We'd a-right whupped them boys."

Shadow Ray slid from the stool and hobbled toward the door. Grabbing the money bag, I looked around to make sure I had put things right for the morning man.

"It's cold, Ray. Want a lift?" I said.

In the mirror, I caught a glimpse of Ray pushing through the door into the shadows outside. The door swung shut, muffling his answer, but I think he said, "I'll make it on my own, Mis-tuh Marlow."

## 12. THE THING THAT SAVED HIM

Cass Pollock was scared of nothing – a good trait, I suppose, except that Cass made *proving* it a full-time job. Take the night he limped into my place clutching an oilskin bundle under his arm. He plopped the bundle on the bar and hoisted a clay-crusted boot onto a stool.

"That's the thing that saved me, Mr. Barkeep, sir."

A few days earlier I had turned twenty-one, so Hansen was finally letting me pour. Between men, a little ribbing is a sign of affection, but Cass wouldn't let it go.

"Get your foot off my stool, Cass," I said.

"Twin Lake boots, Marlow. Best a man can buy."

"Get your Twin Lake boot off my stool. People sit there."

"Clean pants in this berg? Sundays, maybe, but those pants won't be polishing your barstool."

He had a point. Still, without rules where were you?

"You want to try it on, Marlow? Now that you're a full-grown man, you could use a good boot." He paused for effect. "But *my* boot wouldn't fit you, would it? You're only about ... what? An eight? Nine, maybe? You know what they say about men with dainty feet?"

"I know what they say, Cass. Now get that muddy boot down."

"Or what?" he said, turning blustery.

Cass was a restless, sputtering, pressure cooker of a man – noisy and always about to blow. He fought with little provocation, often starting it. That was something he taught me the night I stepped off a Greyhound bus and made my way through a yowling Lake Superior blizzard to the Harbor Bar.

Honoring an old promise, Hansen, the owner, had sprung for a couple of whiskeys. Mellowed, I sat alone at the bar, enjoying the drunken banter of seven buddies squeezed around a table near the glowing, pot-bellied stove. The storm seemed faraway.

*Until* Cass blew in. Scowling and cursing and pacing the floor, he railed against everything and nothing. Goddamm winter. Goddamm snow. Goddamm wind. His commotion was tolerable, but ten was a fiercely unlucky number, and counting Cass, ten we were. Taking my frown personally, however, he shoved his face in mine and spat, "How the wind doth ramm! Sing: Goddamm."

His bizarre performance broke the spell of the bad number. I mean … *Ezra Pound*? When was the last time I heard *any* poet quoted much less Ezra Pound? Half a klick from nothing and what do I hear? Ezra Pound.

Although I had sworn to swear off pissing contests after 'Nam, my head was still screwed on crooked and, besides, some rules you don't choose. Some rules are in the blood and the gut, and without blinking I shot back, "Ezra Pound was bug-ass crazy, mister."

Something saved me: my jungle cameys, the seabag standing erect beside me, what I said, what he heard, my earnestness, maybe … who knows? Whatever it was, Cass passed over. He stomped to the pool table, grabbed up the cue ball, and began to bank it around the cushions.

"Sure he was crazy," he said, more to himself than me. "Poets *have* to be, don't they? And he pulled some rotten tricks, that's for sure. Hell, if I had known the prick, I would've kicked his ass myself. But what does it matter? He wrote some good words. *Good* words."

The sentiment threw me. "They told how the weather was," I said.

Cass snagged the ricocheting cue ball. Tracing circles on it with his thumb, he stood for a moment and listened to the wind ram. "Hey, Hansen," he shouted.

Hansen poked his head from a back room.

"You're wanting help, right? Talk to our boy here. He acts a little queer, but he *might* last."

"Who are you, his agent? Let *him* ask."

Cass tossed me the cue ball. "I'll spot you the break, kid. Let's play."

I lost every game, but I did ask and I *had* lasted, although Cass never once made it easy. I leaned over the bar and shoved his foot off the stool.

He yelped.

"Christ, Cass, you're really hurt!"

"You should see the other guy," he said with a clenched-tooth laugh. I rolled my eyes and he laughed again with enjoyment.

Cass was a good looking man, *particularly* when he laughed. Tall, big-shouldered, bull-necked. Middle-aged in exactly the right way with ruddy cheeks and a white beard. Trouble was, he spoke with a 'wailwoad' impediment and a nasally voice that sounded almost effeminate – qualities hard to reconcile with his looks. Hearing him speak for the first time, strangers often thought he was kidding. To look so solid and sound so fragile was an irony that understandably tickled them. Their chuckles were *hard* on Cass, however. It registered in his face or erupted in the kind of belligerence that greeted me our first meeting.

After a while, I came to think of his appearance as bad luck – one part of him saddling a second, equally fundamental part with an expectancy it could never meet. Still, if you took it the other way, perhaps, given that voice, his appearance was the thing that saved him.

Either way, I decided that the voice explained why Cass was a blowhard, one of those men who can't help but shade the truth. Dangling a magnificent fish in your face, he would lie about its fight, lying needlessly since anyone could see that the fish would have lasted. But Cass had to be the *best* fisherman, the tough*est* boxer, the gam*est* hunter. And that was another strange contradiction, because, in fact, he *was*.

It was as if the Cass you saw – as true as that Cass might be – was nevertheless exaggerated, caricatured, twisted almost grotesque at times by a second truth, some implacable mutagen at the hidden heart of him, an invisible force that contorted him in the way constant winds deform mountains of sand along Lake Michigan despite wind being nothing – nothing to see or hold, anyway, nothing but movement to fill the nothing of a vacuum.

"C'mon, kid, you're *dying* to hear the story," Cass said, shrugging his pack from his shoulders.

I noticed pale welts and fresh, red scratches on his arms, rips in the khaki of his jacket and pants.

"I'm not a kid anymore, Cass."

He positioned his injured foot gingerly on the bar rail.

"That's true ... not since you got your tattoo there," he said, gesturing at the bayonet scar on my forearm. "Well, I have one, too. On my *ass*. From Bastogne. Take a lesson from *that* war. Try to appease madness and lose half your ass!" He elbowed aside the oilskin bundle, leaned on the bar, and ordered a Daiquiri – a Daiquiri for Christ's sake!

"Yup! The Achilles is done for," he said as I shook rum and lime juice. "Bone might be broken, too. But that boot is like armor! Splinted the foot so I could hobble. It saved me all right. That it did."

Cass let the words dangle like a trout fly. And once again he hooked me, since he *did* intrigue me with his stories of huge fish and hunts gone bad and men alone.

"Okay, Cass," I said finally, sliding a stemmed glass across to him. "So tell me. Saved you from what?"

He smiled smugly and grabbed up the glass in his big hand, holding it like a gawky child playing at tea.

"Bear," he said. "Mauled a family at the State Park late this afternoon."

"I heard," I said. "Killed a little girl. Maimed a boy. They doubt he'll walk again."

"What the hell do *they* know," Cass grumbled. He pondered the thought a moment, then began.

"I was returning from an hour jaunt in the Porcupines when I came across the ambulance. Rubberneckers said the bear had less than twenty minutes on me, so I lit out."

"Rifle or bow?"

"Bow was what I had. I followed tracks uphill toward Lake of the Clouds. The bear's trail was erratic. Something was wrong with her. Madness, probably. Animals get that way, just like people; driven to do crazy things for who knows why.

"At the ridge line her tracks vanished on the rock. A mile north I saw rifle-toting Park

Rangers beating the brush alongside the road. Haw! It sure is easy to hunt in the light, isn't it? But, of course, the bear wasn't *in* the light. Scruff marks in the berm led down into this depression.

"Although daylight was left up top, the ridgeline was the horizon down below and the sun had already set. I hadn't thought to re-stock my day pack just to bag a pheasant for dinner and I remembered my flash was dead. Heading off-trail near sunset unprepared is foolhardy, but that bear was sure to kill again. I picked my way down until I found the paw prints. Hand after hand on the young pines, I careened from tree to tree, slip-sliding in the talus near the bottom beside a creek.

"The water was cool and clear, a good trout stream. It wasn't hunger or thirst that drove that bear from her shadowed gorge to a place of light and children. I followed sign downstream, moving hastily, still hoping to kill the bear and get out before nightfall. I was glad I had my pistol with me."

"Hunting pheasants?"

"I always carry it. For insurance, I guess. You never know who or what you'll face in the woods.

Just then, however, I was glad for the bear's sake. An arrow can be slow, especially with bears. They fight it. Grab at it with those big paws, thrash around, drive it deeper. Ever hear the sound a big animal makes dying, Marlow? Same as a dying man or woman, only louder, more pained. A godawful, moaning groan. Angry, sad ... everything at the same time. I *hate* that sound and prefer to end it with a head-shot."

He sipped his drink thoughtfully.

"That was how my father killed himself, you know. A head-shot. I never faulted him for it, although I do wish he had shot my mother first."

I was shocked. Cass rarely mentioned his long-dead father, the town doctor before Doc Phipps. And while he often railed against his mother who was dying of some female cancer, his naked rancor, uttered so deadpan, seemed unnatural, almost deranged.

He tasted his drink again and nodded thoughtfully. "A daiquiri fights itself, doesn't it? Sugar sweet and lime sour. Neither wins. It needs something."

"Like what?"

He sipped and smacked his lips. "Bitterness, I think. For balance. Grapefruit, maybe."

"I don't have grapefruit, Cass."

"I'll bring one next time."

He swirled his glass.

"So, anyway, there I was in a depression, and, believe me, that's a confusing place to be at dusk. Overhead the sky is still blue and the ridge you came from is a bright, yellow ribbon. You know you could still see your way clear up top, but ... where you are? Light fails. Solid things become phantoms. Shadows seem real. Sounds are confined and echo like ghosts."

He tapped the side of his nose with a finger.

"Ever smell a bear, Marlow? Fishy. Fishy like a bad cunt smell." He cackled at my reaction. "What's the matter? Don't like it, you can spit it out ... or maybe you don't know that smell. Haw!"

I said nothing. Why let a storyteller's flaws spoil the story? Cass used both hands to reposition his leg.

"I smelled it all right. I heard it, too," he said. "The satisfied snuffling sounds a bear makes after it eats. I was dead in its stinking parlor. I notched an arrow, crept forward, and—"

He milked a pause with a long sip of his drink.

"What happened?" I said.

"I didn't scream like some sissy, Marlow. I had the will not to scream. That's a trick to learn."

"What the hell *happened*?"

"Trap!" he said, balling a fist. "Goddamm trappers! See why I kick a trapper's ass every chance?"

Cass swiveled on the stool to show me his foot. I leaned over the bar to look.

"See the teeth marks? If not for that boot, those cunt-like jaws would have taken the foot. Damn jaws catch a thing, break it. Suck its power. Make it pitiful. Leave it as pickings for weasels and crows. And Marlow ... the snuffling had *stopped*. No time to free myself, I grabbed up my dropped bow and notched the arrow."

His hands provided downbeats for his words.

"Thickets rustled, leaves crunched. She was coming, Marlow, but the sounds and shadows were lies! Bow drawn, I pivoted around the trapped foot. Over there ... No, there! Finally she charged, straight through the saplings. Branches splintered and popped like firecrackers. Whirling to release, I glimpsed a faltering gait that saved me with a borrowed second. Twang! Got her, Marlow! A damn good midsection shot. She tumbled – momentum carrying her head over feet into the creek. She thrashed, roared, grunted, splashed.

"I broke my bow and almost broke my knife prying against the trap to free my leg. I clawed the pistol from my pack, but by then the thrashing had stopped and the bear was just huffing. Do you know the huffing sounds a big thing makes when it dies, Marlow? Breath is all, and in the end it comes down to that one thing, that one motion, that one sound."

I nodded. I knew.

"Her snout was blood-matted, the blood of those children and, maybe, some of her own. In the last light, I also saw her festering leg – maggots teeming in a trap wound. I wriggled close enough for a sure shot and finished her."

He paused.

"It's funny how a crack of gunshot makes everything so quiet. It deafens you for a moment so the thrashing and the huffing is gone and –

other than a ringing in your ears – you hear
nothing."

He shuddered.

"That silence made me think, Marlow. Think
about losing the foot, I mean. I couldn't count on
rescue, not down there. Who would come except
the sicko who set the trap, returning to gloat
over a rotting trophy? I had to save myself. As
*always*.

"Before the foot ballooned too much, I
fashioned a brace, criss-crossing the laces up and
down the boot top and cinching them tight. Able
to stand that way, I considered my options.

"Follow the stream," I blurted.

"Sure," Cass replied. "Stream is a safer course
in the dark. Fewer pitfalls to trip you when you
can't see. But the stream would take me miles in
the wrong direction – to Lake of the Clouds and
the tourist road no one would travel that late.
Retracing myself, however, I might meet the
rangers I had spotted earlier. Worse call, town
was close. I found a stout branch to lean on and
picked my way upward.

"No moon tonight. Dark fell like a tarp. The
ridge was only a vague line where the stars

stopped. Foot asleep, I couldn't feel the ground, and somewhere high up, I slipped and tumbled. I caught a pine trunk to stop my slide, hugged it with both arms, and wedged myself in on the uphill side. My watch said that I'd been climbing almost two hours!"

He drained the Daiquiri and signaled for another.

"First, you must last," he said. "Ever hear that?"

I shook my head. "It's a good saying though."

I saw him staring at the scar on my forearm as I mixed his drink.

"You have other marks from Vietnam, don't you Marlow?" he said.

I touched my belly and fingered the puckered ridge beneath the shirt-cloth.

"Ones you *can't* touch."

"You should see the other guy, Cass."

He grinned.

"See? You *know*. I knew you knew. I saw it that first day. Just a lost kid, but still cracking wise with a look that told me, however twisted, somewhere back our two paths cross. We've stood at the same spot, Marlow, and either of us could have gone the others' direction."

He laughed at himself.

"Sounds daffy, doesn't it? But that's the kind of hokum you conjure when you're outlasting the dark, when you're looking at nothing and all you see are the shabby things in your head you always see in the dark. I was girded for a long night when I heard the buzz of a motor-scooter engine and saw a single bouncing headlight appear around a bend. Christ, Marlow! The road was fifty yards across from me. I'd veered up the wrong side of the ravine.

"Figuring engine noise would drown my shouts, I fished the revolver from my pack and fired three times in the air. A red brake light flared and the headlight slewed sideways as the scooter skidded to a stop. Doused lights plunged everything back into darkness. I heard scrabbling – taking cover, I guess; I would have!"

"'Lend a hand,' I called."

"I heard a whispered argument and a man crying, 'Why are you shooting?'"

"To signal you. I'm hurt."

"More whispering and a new voice said, 'What's wrong?'"

"A Goddamm *woman*, Marlow! Traipsing around the mountains at night. 'My foot is broken,' I said. 'I was climbing and slipped. I'm stuck.'"

"'What should we do?' she said over mumbled protests."

"Go back to the Ranger station. The road has to cross above me. They can drop a rope."

"How would we find you again in the dark?"

"'Use the damn odometer,' I said."

"More debate, louder, but finally the scooter fired and turned toward town. When it's headlight beam swept the slope behind me, I picked out the ridge line about 10 yards above. Hell, I'd almost made it!

"Settling in, I watched the tail light joggle up the hill and vanish. Suddenly I heard, 'How badly are you hurt?'"

"It was the *woman*! We shouted across the divide."

"What the hell are you doing?"

"Waiting with you."

"Who's on the scooter?"

"'Some boy from town. I'm hitchhiking from Madison, trying for New York. I talked him into showing me Lake of the Clouds by starlight. He probably thought he'd get laid, but he was peeing his pants and about to turn back.' She giggled. 'I think he's scared of the dark. Or *girls*.'"

"'And you're *not* scared,' I said."

"'Of the dark? I'm scared of everything,' she said. 'But there's nothing in the dark.'"

"How about bears, sister? I just killed one."

Abruptly Cass pounded the bar. "She was *silent*, Marlow. I think she was *sad*. For the damn bear! And then she said. 'You must have been frightened.'"

"I made it plain. 'I'm scared of *nothing*.'"

"I saw a match flare and an orange outline of face. 'Weed,' she coughed. 'Sorry can't share. After we save you.'"

"'I don't touch that crap.'"

"She laughed. 'You drink a lot, though, don't you? Everyone I ever knew scared of nothing drank 'til they passed out. Say, what do you look like? I hate talking to people I can't see.'"

"I described myself and she said … get this, she said, 'No … *really*.'"

"'What do you mean … *Really?*' I said."

"Well … your voice sounds much sweeter than that. A little … well, you know … *gentle.*"

"The cunt had me trapped, Marlow! Trapped while she picked me apart."

"'So what do *you* look like, sister?' I said.'"

"Well … I have long, brown hair."

"On your legs?"

"She took another drag and said, 'You're not a nice man, are you?'"

"'I'm a *man,*' I said."

"It must hurt."

"I told you, my foot is broken."

"Not your foot."

"And that, Marlow, was that. I could last ten more stinking yards. Hoisting myself vertical against the pine trunk, I got the good leg under me, and began to inch up the slope."

"'What are you doing?' she said several times. Cascading dirt and stones were making a racket. 'Are you alright? What's happening?'"

"I'm saving *myself.*"

"'Was it something I said?' she giggled."

"She kept on giggling. The dope had her in a tickle fit. She was giggling at *me.*"

Cass gulped his drink.

"Poking my head over the ridge, I saw headlights jouncing toward me. I ducked until they passed, then dragged myself over the edge. Sure enough, I had made my way back to the town road. A long switchback led down to the girl across the canyon.

"'Your little friend just passed,' I shouted. 'You'll see his light in a minute.'"

"I thought you were hurt?"

"'It was a joke, sister. How does it feel to be the butt of a joke?'"

"Don't tell me you left her alone, Cass."

"I'm just a prick, Marlow. I'm *not* inhuman."

He took a swallow of his drink and shook his head.

"Funny ... standing in the rangers' headlights, she looked familiar somehow, like someone I knew years ago, but lost touch with and forgot. She was pretty, too. Nothing like what I'd pictured.

"Rangers threw lights across the ravine to look for me, of course, and, Goddamm, if darkness hadn't exaggerated what I'd called right the first time, a mere hollow, a depression.

Passing it in daylight on two good feet, you'd never guess how hard it would be, blind and wounded, to find your way from the bottom.

"I hacked myself another walking stick and hobbled back toward town, hiding in the trees when they passed me later, swinging spotlights. And here I am," he said smugly. "First, you must last, my man. *First*, you must last."

He shifted his foot again and winced.

"Damn. Doc'll have to cut it off."

"Boot or foot?" I said.

"Boot, wisenheimer, and I hate to lose the thing that saved me. Besides, what good is one boot? Maybe I'll have them bronzed."

Cass swirled his silly drink, guzzled it down, and banged the glass on the bar. I didn't say anything.

"Haw! You're pissed, Marlow. I can feel it."

"Bull!"

"No. You're pissed that I can make it alone and you can't."

"You don't know what I can do, Cass."

"Until you *do* it, *no* one knows," he snapped.

I let it pass. "Do you want a refill?"

"I better see Doc Phipps first. Catch him before he's drunk." He looked around. "Was he in?"

"He was and he is. Same as every night."

"Great. I'll lose the foot anyway."

He smiled somberly.

"It'll feel strange being in that office again. My father called it his storm shelter."

"Doc Phipps' office?"

"Phipps bought it from my mother. The day after my father shot himself. She hated the place. Bitched about it constantly. Said it was wasteful not to see patients at the house. Called it a profligacy, her exact word, *profligacy*. Who in hell talks like that?"

He shook his head muttering the word to himself.

"My old man lasted though. On that one thing, he lasted. He said the office was his refuge from my mother's Goddamm blows. I hid out there, too. See, the walls were covered with thick books that reminded me of bricks. I felt as safe as the third pig behind all those books, even though my father's specimen jars scared hell out of me."

Cass stopped short, seemingly as surprised by the word *scared* as I was.

"I was *little*, okay? ... Look, go ahead and hit me again. Just rum this time. A double."

I poured. Cass downed a hefty slug.

"One jar contained a heart. That spooked me. I mean, an appendix, a tumor ... that's one thing, you know? But a *heart*? Another one had a *real baby* floating inside. I don't think a kid should see something like that. I used to poke at the jar to make her move and I'd ask, 'What do you want, baby?' I always imagined that she answered, 'I want to live.'"

He shook his head sharply.

"Of course, my father was around to explain things in that solid-as-a-brick, Gregory Peck voice of his. I don't think anything scared my father, not even my mother. Oh, she *ruled* him, that's for sure, but she didn't *scare* him. It made me want to be a doctor myself, until I learned the truth. Doctors are too soft. They don't last."

He took a long, deep breath and pushed it out through pursed lips.

"Still … he was all right. He explained the jars and let me use his stethoscope to try to find my heart."

Cass traced a small circle over his breastbone.

"So much for brick houses. The Old Man shot himself right in that examining room. I was six. My sister died not long after."

"I didn't know you had a sister," I said.

"I called her Cassie. And we were close, Marlow. Close like two halves of a whole … like … like that Chinese symbol. You know, the circle with the squiggle in it. Close like that. I *still* miss her. I mean, none of it was Cassie's fault."

"None of what?"

"That our mother was a sick bitch twisted by … by …" He grabbed air with his hands, as if struggling for a grip. "Something festering in her mind, some old wound, something rotten. Hell! Who knows? You can't make sense of madness. Look … best I can figure, she had Cassie, who was the same, but then there was Cass, who was different. Same and different. She couldn't stand it. Same and different. One but two. She just couldn't *stand* it! Like she couldn't stand cocked chairs or clutter. Like she couldn't stand my father's ways.

"There was no *appeasing* her, Marlow! Something about men, I think. Something out of order. Something that stood out. I'll show you a picture someday. Six years old. Long hair in curls. In a *dress*! And the thing is, Marlow, you can't tell if it's me or Cassie! Even *I* don't know!

"Nights we bundled together and prayed for her to die. Cassie died instead – some heart-wasting disease. I was too little to understand, but sometimes I think she was just too soft, thin-skinned, nothing to save her. And sometimes I think she just had to get free. Like my father."

"But *you* stayed."

I'm still not sure why I said it or even what I meant. Hearing it, however, Cass came his closest to hitting me. Closer than the first day or any time since. Cass Pollock was red in the face, no breath at all, rammed by a storm inside – a man about to explode.

"I didn't ... *stay* ... Marlow. I ... *lasted*!" he hissed like an overheated iron boiler venting steam to save itself.

"I am *not* my Goddamm father. I am *not* my Goddamm, tooth-cunted *mother*! And I am *not*—" He swiveled on the bar stool, turning his face away. "I am not my sister."

The movement hiked his trouser leg high enough for me to see his calf, swollen dark blue above the tough hide of the trap-scarred, taut-laced boot. Armor, he had called it, the thing that saved him, and probably he was right. Nevertheless … it had to hurt like hell.

He glowered at people, growling if anyone looked his way. His last words had broken the storm, however, and the growls were merely retreating thunder. After a minute, he stood, grabbed his pack, and limped toward the door.

"I have to wake the Doc," he said.

"What about this," I said, nudging the oilskin bundle.

He halted and turned back.

"Keep it, Marlow. I have a freezer full."

Now I was suspicious. I nudged it again. The bundle left a wet streak like a slug trail. I felt something soft inside, something still a little warm.

"Chippewa believe if you eat a bear's heart, it becomes yours. Try it, Marlow, but take it from experience, they're tough to chew. Toughest Goddammed thing on earth, a bear's heart. Pound it, soak it, stew it ... still like boot leather."

I grabbed the heavy bundle with both hands and chucked it at him. He caught it against his chest, staggering to keep his balance on the bad foot.

"Get that thing out of here! I don't need the heart of a bear, Cass."

"You don't?" He shrugged. "Suit yourself then, but it sure beats nothing."

## 13. TRUE BELIEVER

The pew of barstools stood empty save for Socks, a daytime regular whose immediate excuse was the sweltering summer heat outside. Lost in thought, or maybe just lost, Socks fiddled with his beer mug and muttered to himself. His litany was a soothing white noise, almost a purr. Oddly at peace, I polished the bar and waited for the evening congregation to assemble. Reflected in the lacquered bar-top, an arch of colored bottles rose behind me like a stained glass window.

"Jiminy Christmas!" Socks yelped, slapping his forearm.

"Get him?"

"Oh, I got him all right." He brushed at his arm. "Goddamm black flies! Man, they're the worst I remember. You seen worse, Marlow?"

"Can't say I have."

"It's this Goddamm heat! A hunert 'n two out there. Blacktop's like chewin' gum. My tenny shoes stuck. One-oh-two!"

"One-oh-two," I said.

He pinched the swatted fly between his fingertips. "Flies *love* heat. Sexes 'em up or somethin'. Never *ever* seen no worse."

"Must be the heat," I said.

*"Nasty* boogers." Socks grumbled, eying the fly sourly. "Nasty! Why would God go and make a fly, Marlow? Why?"

"Meanness, maybe?"

Socks flicked away the fly, wiped his fingers on his pants, and resumed his beer mug ritual until the door opened.

"You're lettin' the flies in!" Socks barked at a reluctant figure standing silhouetted against the light."Were you raised in a barn? Shut the— Oh say, Tommy, it's you! Marlow, it's Tommy!"

A small, frail man – poor match for the hellish weather – struggled onto a stool. Swallowed in a baggy, borrowed suit, wayward hair greased in place, he propped his elbows on the bar and cupped his face in his hands as if praying.

Socks switched stools to pat the man's back. "Sorry, Tommy. I feel plain rotten."

Tommy nodded dumbly.

"I'da come," Socks continued, "but ... well, you know, you said—"

"You guys were the old life. Didn't seem right, you to be there."

Tommy sighed. His breath whooshed in his steepled palms like wind in a cave.

"You okay, Tommy?" I said.

Nodding as if deliberating, he lowered his hands.

"Give me something, Marlow."

"Club soda? Ginger ale?"

"No. Give me something."

"Tommy! Tommy!" Socks exclaimed, shooting me a glance. "One day at a time. One day at a time, man."

"Southern Comfort," said Tommy. "Straight up."

"I know how you're hurtin'," Socks persisted, "but that's no reason to—"

"Know how I'm hurting, Socks? When did you bury a wife? When?"

"Ain't buried nobody lately, Tommy."

"Then stick a cork in it."

Socks squeezed Tommy's shoulder. "C'mon, man! Time was, figured we was gonna bury *you*. You got two years now. You got your job back at the mill. Got your license back. Lemme call whoosis, that, uh … *sponsor* guy."

Tommy shrugged away the hand.

"You serving, Marlow, or what?"

I selected a polished, old-fashioned glass, chose a bottle from the back-bar, and poured.

"Fill it!" Tommy said impatiently.

I topped off the glass and left the bottle on the bar. Tommy peered hesitantly into the amber liquid as if at a foreboding augury.

"Two years. Two years for what?"

"Two years you ain't in the lock-up seeing snakes," said Socks. "Two years you ain't bringin' up blood."

"That was Grace, Socks! Like … like she fished me out of Hell. S..she …"

Tommy's head dropped. His shoulders shook, but he made no sound. I reached across the bar. He reared back and grabbed the glass.

"One day at a time? Well, here's to this day and the next day and all the days in Hell to come."

"That don't drown the fire," urged Socks.

"Says the captain of the bucket brigade."

"Just let him be, Socks," I said. "One fool is bad enough."

"I'm worse than a fool, Marlow."

"Not talking about you, Tommy. Talking about Grace. She thought she could count on you."

Glass at his lips, Tommy froze.

"Death, Marlow. That's *all* we can count on!"

"Then that's that. Another fool gone to worms."

"Sonovabitch!" Tommy groaned, setting the glass down hard. Half his drink sloshed onto the bar. I tugged the towel from my belt to blot the spill.

"Is that what you believe, Tommy?"

"NO! Not ... not like *that*."

"Then what *do* you believe?"

Tommy slumped as if some prop had slipped.

"I believed in Grace."

"So life is senseless now?"

"Where's the sense of cancer?"

"I suppose God is dead, too. Maybe never was."

Tommy teetered, ancient prohibitions warning him back from some abyss.

"We..ll, didn't say *that*. Gotta be a God, but—"

"But what? He bungled this one? What?"

Not one to know his feelings or squeeze feelings into words, Tommy flailed his hands. I slid his glass out of reach.

"I just don't understand, Marlow. Why Grace? Why Grace and not—" He pounded the bar. "I was nothing. I'm still nothing! Grace was ... She was ... She was *special*, Marlow. She was an angel."

Socks opened his mouth to interject, but I held up a hand. He shrugged and drank his beer.

"So, maybe she's home now, Tommy," I said. "*Really* home."

Tommy's eyes seemed drawn to the church-window pattern reflected in the bar-top.

"Wish I could believe it, Marlow."

"You said you believe in God, right?"

His answer echoed from a well so deep he could never know the source.

"I ... I believe in God," he said.

"Then somehow, some way, things make sense."

"*Gotta* make sense!" he whispered.

"Sensible thing is she's with Him now, right?"

"I can't believe she's just ... *gone*."

"Odds are, if she's with Him, she's still watching over you. Believing in you."

Tommy looked up. "You think? You think it's true?"

I nodded.

"You've lived a bit, Marlow. You've seen things. You read books and you *know* things." His voice grew stronger like words from a parched throat after a cool drink of water. "You think? You really think?"

"What I *know*, Tommy, is you need to believe."

"I want to believe," Tommy said. "I want to believe so bad!" He closed his eyes and took a long, deep breath. "She's with God, now, Marlow," he said finally.

"You can count on it," I said.

He opened his eyes again. "She's done with pain. Done with pills that make her sick. She's *home* now."

I nodded.

"She's watching over me, like she always did. Helping me do better. One day at a time." He smiled and pushed the half-empty glass across the bar. "I almost lost it there, Marlow. Thanks."

"Thank Grace," I said.

He stood, leaned over the bar, and grasped my shoulders with both hands, as close to a hug as he could come with the bar between us.

"God bless you, Marlow."

He groped in his pocket for a few bills, slapped them on the bar, and turned to leave.

"God bless both of you!" he said, pushing through the door. Hot air rushed in like heat off an opened firebox.

"Well looky-looky-looky," Socks snickered when I dinged the register. "Teacher says every time you hear a bell, an angel gets his wings!"

I separated my tip from Tommy's bills, stashed the tip in my shirt pocket, and deposited the rest in the drawer.

"You don't believe it, Socks?"

"Jumpin' Jesus, Marlow!" he said, pausing to drain his mug. "*You* don't believe it neither."

"I don't?"

"I've heard you talk there ain't no God. Heard it with my own ears."

"Your own ears," I drawled, refilling his mug.

Socks slurped the head off the fresh beer and downed half to chase the heat.

"She's home now. She's watchin' over you," he said mockingly. "*Haw!* You don't believe a word you fed him."

"You think? You really think?"

"See? You was puttin' him on."

"Maybe I'm putting you on, Socks."

"Christ on a pogo stick! Maybe you don't believe nothin'."

"More's the pity," I said.

I lifted Tommy's glass and tossed back the remainder. The drink burned like iodine on a raw wound. I poured more from the bottle close to hand.

"Say, uh … easy there, Marlow. One at a time, man."

"Who's counting," I said.

I swirled the liquor and stared into the tiny whirlpool. Upending the shot, I saw a face before me like a vision, like an augury. But it was only my own face reflected in the bottom of the empty glass. I banged the glass back onto the bar.

"C'mon, Marlow. Not *this* again. You got a long spell till closin'."

"I believe you, Socks," I said, reaching for the bottle.

## 14. PRESENT PERFECT

The English teacher was a gray, inconspicuous, little man, an every-night-but-Saturday regular who, nevertheless, shunned elbow-rubbing at the bar in favor of the corner booth where he could sip his single drink unmolested. Awaiting his turn, he stood off to himself.

"You're up, Mr. Molina," I shouted, spotting his hesitancy when a couple vacated the booth. And since he was a man of habit, I reached for the sherry.

"Not tonight, Mr. Marlow!" he exclaimed, hurrying to the bar. "Thank goodness you haven't poured. I *would* have paid, of course. I should have spoken sooner."

"No harm, no foul. What'll it be?"

Small and made even smaller by a cocoon of empty space he wove around himself, the English teacher rose on tiptoes to lean across the bar-top.

"Do you have Champagne?" he whispered.

"I, uh … suppose so," I said. I stooped, opened the fridge, and shuffled bottles to reach the old maids. "We're in luck. Let's see. A New York State Cordon Bleu and … Wow, Mumm's!"

"Oh my! I'm no oenophile. Are they quite different?"

"Mumm's is French, Mr. Molina. Thirty dollars different."

"Oh my!"

He touched a finger to his lip, mentally ticking off necessities he could forego.

"It's the book, not the cover, right?"

He nodded. "Sage advice, Mr. Marlow. Very well … Cordon Bleu it is!"

He thumped the bar, but shrank from his exclamation point and scurried to the horseshoe shaped booth. Stealing a nervous glance at the crowd, he burrowed in one side.

An ill November wind was blowing good business my way. Searching for an ice bucket, I poured a dozen refills. Nick Andropolis, mate on a local fishing boat, shoved out his empty mug.

"Goddamm shame about the VA hospital, ain't it," he said.

"What's that?"

"You ain't heard? The government tore it down!"

I was silent.

"The *big* one. In Detroit. You was there, too, right?"

I shrugged.

"So what're we s'posed to do now?"

"It's a day's ride, Nick. You haven't been back in thirty years."

"The point is the point, man. We can't count on it no more."

"Then I'd stop counting on it."

I filled the ice bucket, crunched in the Champagne bottle, and carried it over to the booth. The English teacher sat polishing his rimless spectacles. Replacing the eyeglasses, he surveyed the noisy menagerie.

"Everyone here tonight is a former student," he mused. "Except you, of course."

Mr. Molina was a fixture at the high school long before I came north.

"Mr. Andropolis attended my very first class."

"Nick? Nick looks old enough to be *your* teacher," I said, untwisting the wire bail.

"Some burn while others rust, Mr. Marlow. Mr. Andropolis was an Odysseus, scorched by far-flung exploits. Observe his broken nose, those tattoos, his scarred fists. I was but Telemachus, far from battle."

"They also serve, Mr. Molina."

"Yes, yes ... I'm sure my waiting served. I forged agreement among my subjects ... and verbs. I preserved the union ... of infinitives. I rescued the occasional dangling participle. The home fires, however, do not scorch."

Silently the old man kneaded his knobby hands. I wrapped the sweaty champagne bottle in a towel to ease out the cork.

"My boys and girls dislike me," he said abruptly. "They call me names behind my back and write terrible things on the lavatory walls. I'm not ... not *that way*, you know."

"Kids are kids, Mr. Molina."

"I understand. I *do*. Young people see the trodden path of grammar as a rut, as something to be escaped. They frolic about, lost, rather than—" He sighed. "Forgive me, Mr. Marlow. I am by nature a pedant."

The bottle gave a muted pop.

"Oh, my!" he gasped. "Such a gay sound."

I poured, allowed the bubbles to subside, filled his glass to the brim, and screwed the bottle back into the ice bucket.

"Cheers, Mr. Molina," I said, turning to leave.

The old man touched my arm. "I ... I believe Champagne spoils quickly, correct? It's not something one saves?"

"Only in memory."

"Then, perhaps ..." He cleared his throat. "You have always been kind to me, Mr. Marlow. You dissuade my former charges from teasing and permit me my nightly hour undisturbed. W..will you share a toast? Just this once?"

I glanced back at the bar. He blanched.

"How *thoughtless* of me. So blustery an evening. You're busy."

"No one's dry. Hold on."

I grabbed a goblet from behind the bar and slid into the booth. Mr. Molina wriggled sideways to divide the space fairly.

"Allow me," he said, removing the bottle from the bucket to fill my glass.

"So what's the occasion?"

His color rose, a secret pleasure bubbling from some hidden reservoir.

"My story was published today!"

"You're kidding! Congratulations." I clinked his glass. "You never said you were a writer."

"Oh, I'm not, I'm not. What's the adage ... everyone has a story to tell? I finally told mine, that's all. Would you like to see it?"

"Absolutely! I've never known a real author."

Blushing again, he withdrew a blue, card-stock covered pamphlet from inside his coat and carefully smoothed the crease.

"It's just a little magazine," he said, "*Gogebic College Review*. And a tiny, tiny story. I ... I could *read* it to you?"

I disliked being read to, but an urgency in his voice testified to the importance of *speaking* the words, as if seeing the words *heard* mattered more than seeing them in print, as if writing were merely a ruse to allow telling.

"Well ... Sure. Sure, go ahead. A few minutes won't hurt."

He swallowed a gulp of champagne and opened the trembling booklet directly to the proper page.

"*Still Life,*" he began. "By Terry Molina."

He took a deep breath and plunged in.

"On Saturdays Tristan Morrow beheld color, which is not to suggest that he was otherwise color-blind. Color-blindness, he knew, was a sex-linked, chromosomal abnormality inherited from one's mother and Morrow had passed every test. He *perceived* color plainly enough, but ordinarily ignored it. On Saturdays, however, color suffused his existence in the way dark ink spreads through white blotter paper revealing cyan and magenta and yellow at the edges. Saturday colors were redolent and raucous. They shouted, they reeked, they prodded. Red inflamed, green tingled with a mossy softness, orange squealed, purple clamored, brown smacked of morning-mouth. Saturday blue tolled.

"This was Dana's doing. Dana was an art teacher for whom colors were more than mere attributes, but things in themselves. Although Morrow envied Dana's grasp of color, he could only approximate that understanding with his own English-teacher notions. Color was a *language*, a tongue in which Dana was natively fluent. Morrow knew the primer words, but used them as would a toddler – nominatively, with no inkling of syntax."

Clutching his little magazine, Mr. Molina ploughed through the words. Every few sentences he glanced up to observe my reactions. His head rose from the page with the rhythm of a swimmer taking air.

"Morrow's awakening to this strange language had occurred thirty years earlier at a teachers' conference in New York City. Seated in a crowded symposium, he saw Dana sidestepping down his row. He lowered his eyes and prayed she would overlook him."

"'Hi, Tristan!' she chirped, plopping into an empty seat beside him. 'Thought it was you.'"

"Although Dana taught at the same small, Michigan high school as did Morrow, they spoke rarely. Morrow was an awkward man who avoided all but essential conversation. Passably well-spoken counseling students or reading lecture notes, when stripped of his teacher guise, he was lost for words – or more precisely, lost for grammar."

"Morrow imagined social fluency as yet *another* language, one planted in the brain before birth. In himself, the seed of that language had failed to germinate or its flower had early wilted. He cast his problem as analogous to his mother's aphasia. A stroke had left her fluent with jabberwocky. Her thoughts emerged jumbled and bungled. Unable to understand the words of others or herself – suddenly a stranger in a strange land – she ultimately took refuge in terminal silence."

"Morrow saw himself as *socially* aphasic. Although he needed conversation in the way a subject needs a verb, his befuddled attempts at human contact were inevitably misunderstood. Likewise, he misinterpreted and over-analyzed the actions of others. Fortunately – much as blindness fosters acute hearing – Morrow's loneliness had nurtured a keen sensitivity to the distress his handicap caused others. Considerate of that distress, he withdrew behind dark glasses of emotional reserve and self-effacing diffidence that rendered him almost invisible."

"Hence Dana's greeting jarred him, dislodging his usual mask of chilly reticence. He gave a graceless, blinking nod. His awkwardness was compounded by her tardiness. Morrow would as apt plunge needles into his eyes as make such a spectacle of himself. Dana, however, was among those unfathomable 'late people' who could breeze into a staff meeting wearing a 'how-foolish-of-you-to-start-without-me' smile."

"Crossing her legs, she leaned toward him and said, 'What's a nice guy like you doing in a place like this?'"

"Morrow was panic stricken. Not only had she disrupted the lecture with her entrance, she had addressed him aloud. Blame for her unconscionable conduct might fall upon *him*. And what did she mean, a place like this? It was a reputable talk on advances in pedagogy. Why should he *not* be here? And nice? Did she *really* think that he was nice? Perhaps the remark was facetious. Or even *sarcastic*. Swept by alarms of struggle or flight, Morrow froze."

"The speaker at the podium, a Midwestern principal, discussed iterative evocation of arithmetical mnemones, which Morrow (ill-versed in mathematics) took to mean reciting times tables. Dana's metal bracelets jingled as she crossed and uncrossed her arms."

"'You *can't* be listening to this twaddle,' she said, barely lowering her voice."

"A gentleman to Morrow's right hissed, 'Please ask your lady-friend to SSHHHHH!'"

"'Why should he?' Dana snapped, pointing at the man's notebook. 'You're just doodling anyway.'"

"Morrow covered his face. Dana laughed."

"'C'mon, Tris, I think we stumbled into a *Gramps for Goldwater* rally.' Morrow peeked between his fingers. Dana stood and extended her hand. Her bracelets winked in the dimmed light. 'C'mon! Before they draft you.'"

"Springing to his feet, Morrow seized Dana's hand, but immediately let go, fearful that he had squeezed too hard. Dana trapped his fluttering hand between her palms like a boy catching a dayfly. Together they sidled down the row of folding chairs toward an exit."

"'Make up your mind,' whispered a shriveled, prune of a man."

"'I *have!*' exclaimed Morrow."

"Eyes turned toward him, a *sea* of eyes, a surge of attention sure to drown him. Astonishingly, however, the wave receded. Eyes ebbed back to the speaker. The prunish man looked down and said nothing."

"Tumbling in a torrent of emotions, Morrow burst with Dana from the conference room. Still holding hands, they scampered down the marble staircase, crossed the lobby and plunged through a revolving door into a pool of Fifth Avenue pedestrians waiting for a signal."

"'You told him!' she chortled."

"I ... I suppose I did."

"'Did you see his face? He turned purple!'"

"Morrow released her hand. 'Listen, Miss Farber, why ... why are you doing this?'"

"'Why? Because it's April. Because the park is bursting with golden-green. Because life is too short to spend *any* of it in that awful, brown room.' Laughing, she flung out her arms and wheeled. Her hair glinted with sunshine. 'Hey! Here's an idea. The Met has a fabulous modern art collection. Let's go!'"

"'I don't know much about art and I don't trust *modern* art at all,' he said."

"'Loosen up, Tris. Rigor mortis is setting in. C'mon! We're strangers here. I don't know anyone and I bet you don't either. We have a day. Why spend it in brown when there are rainbows to see? Why spend it alone? I don't like being alone.'"

"Morrow looked down."

"Dana grabbed Gray's hand again as a swell of pedestrians swept them into the crosswalk. Scampering, almost skipping, she dragged him along."

"'I would have chosen red for go,' she said. 'Red for go and I think, maybe … blue for stop? Yes, *blue*! Blue should mean stop. What do you think?'"

"The question was absurd in the way modern art was absurd. What profit lay in seeing things as they were not. Green was go and that was that. He turned to protest, but words dissolved in the most liquid gaze he had ever encountered, a look that offered joyous immersion in the might and ought to be. What was it about her face? Some attribute that ... *Blue*! Her eyes were an almost blinding blue."

"'Blue for stop?' she persisted."

"Morrow felt the movement of facial muscles he rarely noticed. 'No,' he said, smiling. 'Not stop. Blue should mean *go*.'"

"Okay, I'm in! Let's start a petition. We'll need a catchy name. An acronym."

"Northerners Undermining Traffic Safety?"

"'Cool beans!' she laughed. 'Tris likes to *play*. Who knew?'"

"Waltzing down Fifth Avenue, they paused to examine a scarlet pennant, a blue bird, a purple sign, the green moss that had insinuated itself into the gray stones of the park wall."

"Color is important to you,' he said as they strolled.

"'I don't think of it as important or unimportant. I paint so I—'"

"'Let's do an experiment.' He stepped behind her. 'No, no! Look straight ahead. What am I wearing?'"

"'Gray,' she answered smugly."

"That's all? Aren't artists *observers*?"

"'Gray is the *theme*,' she said, sounding miffed. 'Your tie is burgundy with gray accents. And those brown shoes don't make it.'"

"He glanced at his feet. 'Oh, my! I was assured of their quality. Well ... no matter. Two-button or three-button coat?'"

"She turned impatiently. 'Okay, three-button. So?'"

"'So that's my point! I would have answered a suit. If asked for details, I would have said a three-button suit. I see a suit that happens to be gray. You see gray that happens to be a suit. Isn't that fascinating?'"

"'No biggie,' she chuckled. *'Everything* about me is fascinating!'"

"'I agree,' he blurted."

"'Why, Tris, you little flirt! Your red face goes perfectly with that burgundy tie.' She fluttered his tie and grabbed his arm when he almost fled. 'Tris! Tristan, look at me,' she said. 'Don't you know I'm flirting with *you*?'"

Waving his beer mug, Nick growled that I should let Old Man Molina grade his own papers. The little man slammed shut his magazine as if to protect the contents. I told Nick to draw himself one on the house and waited. The English teacher resumed.

"At the museum, Dana introduced Morrow to Matisse and Chagall, Hopper, Miro and Klee. Morrow strove to see the canvases other than as a grammarian and came closest when Dana enlisted his participation in a finger-painting workshop teeming with noisy schoolchildren."

"'Watch the kids,' she said. '*They* know. They're born knowing plane and color. Adults wring the art from them squeezing color between lines.'"

"'Lines make the picture,' Morrow insisted."

"'Oh, *really?*'"

"She encircled him from behind with her arms and forced his fingers into mounds of cold, gooey paint daubed with tongue-depressors from screw-top jars. Folding colors together – her hands guiding his – they created mountains and clouds and rills, planted fields of yellow on green, carved paths of orange through a wilderness of purple, swelled waves of red across an ocean of blue."

"'Now what was that about *lines?*' she said."

"The question disturbed him. Or, perhaps, it was her arms. Morrow had never been embraced before except by his mother. Careful not to break the circle, he turned."

"The blue of Dana's eyes – a hue Morrow fancied as that of a tropical sea – whispered *Go!* He let himself be drawn, as if on some propitious tide."

"'Look, Mommy!' exclaimed a schoolchild, pointing a paint-smeared finger. 'They're going to *kiss.*'"

"Morrow felt a jolt as if tethered on an anchor."

"'Well … ?' said Dana."

"Beyond his safe harbor stretched oceans, unmarked and boundless. How lost he would be there. How unable to find home. Morrow sighed and seemed to hear in his ebbing breath the melancholy withdrawal of a tide untaken."

"'Lines are superfluous,' he conceded, stepping out of Dana's arms. 'For an *artist.*'"

"'That's a start!' she said, beaming with the satisfaction of a scientist who had proved her hypothesis. And for thirty years, Morrow's most-treasured moments had been memories of that smile."

"Of course, his words were actually an *end*. Nothing bloomed of that Saturday in New York. Returned to the carefully drawn lines of Morrow's workaday life, he and Dana were but acquaintances. Although he spoke more easily to her than others, he did so rarely. Her invitations to this and that, meeting with rejection, ultimately ceased. When she departed for San Francisco that Fall, Morrow's only link was a small, black-and-white photograph published annually in the teachers' association registry. The photograph created two asynchronous worlds. In the world reflected in his shaving mirror, Morrow's face decayed with the imperceptible but implacable progression of an hour hand. In *her* world, Dana aged in giant steps as an old photo, used for years, abruptly yielded to one more recent. And one year, her photo vanished. A clerk at the registry told Morrow that Dana had died. How she had lived, he was unable to say. Shortly thereafter, Morrow began his Saturday visits."

"As usual on Saturday, Morrow stopped first at the gate to purchase a bouquet of flowers. He chose colors thoughtfully, remembering that Dana had said some combinations tolled like chimes while others screeched like chalk on a blackboard. Winding down a blacktop line dividing green planes of lawn beneath a blue bowl of sky, he parked at his usual spot."

"When first he began his visits, Morrow had searched faithfully for a marker that bore the same given name, the same approximate year of birth. Time passing, he realized that one lost life was much the same as another. Hence, now, when his hip ached or when snow made the trek arduous, he accepted any grave."

"Sitting, he placed the spray of flowers beneath a headstone – today the grave of someone named Terry, a man or woman whose life was summed by the hyphen linking two dates. Morrow spoke neither to Dana nor to Terry during his vigil. Saturday tributes were in a wordless language, unvoiced hymns to something more bleak than death – to never having been born. Studying the flowers, he rearranged them in his mind to create a still life, a frozen moment whose colors were more true, more real, more lasting than those of the cut flowers themselves, weak things that would wilt and wither and fade."

Mr. Molina closed the little magazine and returned it to his pocket.

"It's very good," I said.

"Really? You liked it?"

"I did. It's very, very good."

Beaming, the teacher raised his glass to drain a final drop. He placed bills on the table and stood.

"Hold on, Mr. Molina. You have change."

"Keep it. For service above and beyond, as they say."

I swirled the champagne bottle. "And a couple glasses yet."

"I draw the line at one."

"C'mon! Celebrate."

"No, Mr. Marlow. That way madness lies." As if weighing the thought, however, he glanced toward the bar. "But perhaps I can trouble you for an additional indulgence. Would you share the remainder with Mr. Andropolis? Tell him it's a belated *cum laude* for his extra-curricular achievements."

He was tipsy. And since he was, I said, "Your story. Is it true?"

"Is it true? ... Do you mean, autobiographical?"

I nodded.

"I've not been to New York City, Mr. Marlow."

"Of course," I said. "It's just a story. See you tomorrow, Mr. Molina."

"Never on Saturday," he corrected. "Sunday."

The English teacher toddled to the entrance, but paused to look back at the booth. "Solo celebrations are so very, very dreary," I heard him say to himself. "Yes! This *has* been fun." Heads turned when he opened the door to leave, but only in response to the noisy wind.

"Champagne!" Nick cackled when I returned to the bar with the ice bucket and glasses. "You and Old Man Molina get engaged?"

I poured a glass, pushed it toward Nick, and emptied the bottle into my own glass.

"Drink up. He called you an Odysseus."

"What's that s'posed to mean?"

"It's Greek."

"Yeah? *That* figures."

I hoisted my glass. "We're toasting Mr. Molina's story. *Still Life.* It's about a girl he liked a long time ago who—"

"Girl? I freakin' doubt it, Marlow. He's queer."

"Why do you have to—"

"I'm just *saying*! Look ... Molina is a dyed-in-the-wool mommy's boy. His old lady was a English teacher, too. Even *worse.* All their do's and don'ts, those lines you couldn't cross 'stead of just saying what comes natural. Two peas in a pod. I blame 'em both for me joining the Navy.

"Besides ... I seen him once myself. Stayed late after practice. Heard laughing in the art room and peeked in. Him and this nancy-boy art teacher was playing with paint. Guy had his arms wrapped around Molina and they was getting all moony till my eyeballing gave it the kibosh."

The jukebox played some song everyone knows but no one remembers.

"Yesiree! Him and his old lady even lived together 'til a few years ago when a couple of strokes pretty much scrambled the biddy. Molina had to put her in a home over to Marquette. I know a guy what works there. Says the old man comes every Saturday evening with flowers. Just sits with that vegged-out, ball-buster, not saying a word. Go figure."

I lifted my glass for one last toast.

"To poets and their lies," I said.

"Whatever," Nick said, downing the wine and smacking his lips.

A howl from the doorway announced new business. Nick frowned.

"That's the Witch stirring," he said.

"A little early, isn't it?"

"It's the Witch."

"Are you going out tomorrow?"

"Yeah … Yeah, I'm going out … " he said pensively. Suddenly he crossed himself. "Listen … Molina gave me Champagne and all I had for him was bile. God sends bad luck for such as that, so irregardless of my spite, them two deserve fair due as family. Molina is a good son and his old lady must've been a good Mama, because, for sure, he loved her."

I considered it for a moment, trying to imagine a grammarian's palette.

"He *has* loved her, Nick. He has always loved her." I corrected. "Present perfect."

## UNCOUNTED:  TIME OUT OF MIND

Turns out, that talking-ass, *other*-timer had my number. I've remembered his stories for thirty years now. And count it strange, but the story I remember most is one he told *about* remembering.

He said, "Sometimes I remember something when maybe the truth is, I only *think* I remember it. Bleary, jigsaw memories of times in the Veterans' Hospital or times I was too drunk to walk. Even those crystalline memories of gun-lit seconds when I was so piss-myself scared every elephant ear leaf is flash-etched in my head like an image on high speed film. They all seem real enough, those memories – I mean, I *remember* them, right? But what if they're only stories I've been told or ones I've told myself so often it *feels* like they happened. Memories like that can be a way to forget something else, or so I've heard, anyway."

He pondered the idea.

"That's a tough nut, isn't it? Memories to help *forget*. I guess it's like those needles they stick you with to relieve pain."

"Acupuncture?"

"Yeah. Acupuncture. Another mystery to me. How can pain help pain?"

And then he told this story.

"I remember dressing for school one sunshiny morning when I couldn't have been more than five because we moved about that time and this was in the first house – the first I remember, anyway – the tall house, red-brick like the third pig's house, the house with the giant, weepy-willow tree and the long, long side yard where I knocked baseballs over the fence into the street, or at least I remember doing that.

"Wednesday was share day in kindergarten. You know … a day you brought in something with a story to it – a toy soldier, a saved letter, arrowheads, a magic slate. I liked share day. I liked to tell stories.

"But days run together at that age – you don't quite have a handle on day names yet – so I asked my father what day it was, and he said *Tuesday*. Day names were still like the alphabet to me – one long word I whooshed out in a single breath, and I thought I remembered people calling *yesterday* Tuesday.

"Mondaytuesday..*tuesday*?..wednesday-thursdayfridaysaturdaysunday sounded strange, like ABC..*C*..D, so I said 'How come?'"

"My father had forgotten childhood. Everyone does; we *need* to. His face puckered as it frequently did when my ways were peculiar to him – say, when I counted steps or fence posts or telephone poles or when I preferred two nickels to one quarter. My mother just giggled – that little-girl giggle she gave when she felt one-up on my father – and she said, 'It's *Wednesday*, Lyndon.'"

"She understood what my father didn't: how *completely* I believed him. If he said there were two Tuesdays, I merely wondered why.

"Today, that moment seems perfectly real, and mostly I'd say it's true. On the other hand, my parents *loved* that story – something about the innocent belief of *'how come'* and maybe something about its loss, too. I remember them repeating it to every new friend or acquaintance, embarrassing me with it at every gathering. They told the story at parent-teacher days and at my graduation from high school and at the garden party when I shipped out for Vietnam. And if they were alive and here now, I bet they'd still be telling it – telling it to *you* as I just did.

"And the thing is, I remember the *telling* so well, I can't decide if I remember it happening, or only *think* I remember it because I remember the *story*. Funny how something *told* can feel so real inside, so beyond doubt, so *unquestionable* that you'd stake your life on its truth. I mean, another time, another place – like right here, right now with you, or wherever, some jungle, a desert, a mountainside – you'd literally *stake your life on it*. And all it is, is someone's story. What's the name for a memory like that? I forget, but I know there's a name."

Me remembering thirty years later that old madman remembering people from his *own* way-back-when feels full-on weird. I see myself seeing *him* see *them*, and it's like I'm looking in a mirror *reflecting* a mirror. That's what it is now, isn't it? *All* of the way-back-when times, even the real ones – just a fading column of reflected reflections.

Take the *other timer* himself – heavy drinker, light sleeper. Thirty more years would be stretching it. Or if he *did* last? No family to police things, nothing to save him, he's probably shaking in some piss-stinking old folks home, or maybe back in a VA hospital slumped in a Goddamm day room chair, and if he's thinking at all, it's probably about catching a Greyhound.

Bag that noise! I'll just remember him still tending bar at ninety.

Like I imagine I'll be.

Anyway, damned if I didn't know the word he'd forgotten. I remembered it from a psychology class my one year of junior college.

"Screen memory," I told him.

"What's that?" he said. Already his question was fading.

"A memory to help forget. You wanted to know what it's called."

"That's it!" he said, snapping his fingers. "Like acupuncture. That's *just* what it's called. A screen memory."

# ABOUT THE AUTHOR

Besides *Another Time* – a story-cycle about a castaway Vietnam veteran who finds safe harbor as a bartender in a small, northern Michigan town – Joseph Hullett's fiction includes the novel *Killing Rain, Killing Fire,* and numerous short stories, some of which are collected as *Men with Women.* His new novel *Philosopher's Stone* is slated for publication in Fall 2013.

His plays, staged from New York to Los Angeles, have earned accolades that include the Julie Harris Award, the Ventana Play Award, Silver Medal in the Pinter Review Prize and finalist selection for both the Arts and Letters Drama Prize and the Heideman Award.

A psychiatrist, Hullett lives in southern California near Camp Pendleton ... within earshot of the cannon fire.

BONUS SAMPLE PAGES

# Philosopher's Stone

Is there an alchemy for leaden grief? Fast-forward from *Killing Rain, Killing Fire* to the tenth anniversary of Veronica's death where private investigator Pete Pinel stands at the dead-end of a long goodbye.

## Chapter One

The night the madman came, I was alone in the dark. On the desk behind me lay a crumpled eviction notice and my account book.

What was the profit?

I had swiveled my chair toward the window because I was tired of the ledger. In dwindling twilight its tiny numbers had coalesced into an inescapable bottom line. When your sole livelihood is private investigation and you stop looking for cases, refuse those that find you, and forfeit ones you can't refuse, you end up broke.

Maybe it's an occupational hazard. I couldn't name a rich private detective except Pinkerton or Hammett. And Pinkerton made it a business rather than a calling while Hammett lost the calling, so I ignored them. Besides, they both died, and dying is dead broke – a bankruptcy we all go through. I pictured a balance sheet – assets minus liabilities, for which the final entry is always zero.

Stiff from sitting so long, I stood, walked to the window, and fired a cigarette. Misty rain blurred the squat San Dismas buildings. Orange County seemed to be slipping away in low, dark clouds like smoke from smudge pots that once protected long-gone Orange Groves. I lifted the sash to feel rain on my skin.

Four floors below crawled a slow procession of cars, headlights staring, windshield wipers blinking back the drizzle. Across Main, in front of a hole where a demolished bank once stood, a line of black umbrellas waited for a bus. When the bus came, a lone figure scurried from the rear door, ducked his head, and darted across traffic toward shelter.

## Philosopher's Stone

A gust of wind curled the cigarette smoke and watered my eyes. Blinking, I cursed myself yet again for surrendering to a dependence I had conquered till the day Ronnie died.

No. Not *that* day. Until her funeral. Ten years ago. Exactly ten years ago. Armistice Day. A day like this one.

Dark.

Wet. Lonely.

Final.

Anniversaries resurrect memories. I felt mine pounding against their reliquary. I flipped my cigarette out the window and watched it arc downward to die in the rain. Lights winked on and off. Glistening streets reflected meaningless geometric patterns. Wind and traffic hissed and groaned in my ears like noise in a void. The weariness I felt had no name.

Withdrawing from the window, I opened the small refrigerator on the vanity counter and removed the last Sapporo. I pried off the bottle-cap and swallowed two ... three ... four times. I didn't feel it. I hadn't felt the others. I sat the bottle on the counter top and poked another cigarette between my lips

The ancient USMC Zippo I carried was the one
Jesus bought at boot camp and treasured like a
*Phi Beta Kappa* key. I ran my thumb over the
once-gold eagle-globe-and-anchor insignia long
since worn smooth and silvery.

I imagined him in his wheelchair bellyaching
about me sitting in the dark. His voice had faded
less in memory than his face, so the clearer part
was the growled, "Pull your sorry self together,
*cabron!*"

Jesus could say whatever he wanted. When
heaven was falling, he stood with me. Suddenly I
longed to tell him the good-bye he never heard,
the one I uttered over his broken body when the
gang who murdered Ronnie ran him down.

The flashback seemed to breach some stony
crust confining an eternally molten rage. I
needed to kill the killers again. I needed it like
water. Like air. I needed to chase them to hell
and kill them *one last time*; kill them so they
stayed dead.

Closing my eyes, I took deep breaths until my
hands steadied enough to flick the lighter and
fire the cigarette in my mouth. I let the lighter
burn for a moment, contemplating a ghostly coil

of sooty smoke writhing above the yellow flame. When I snapped shut the lighter and dropped it back in my pocket, it felt hot against my thigh. The heat inside me, however, had subsided again beneath the cold, stone crust.

In the gloom of the unlighted office, the mirror above the vanity reflected only my murky shadow. When I drew on the cigarette, the flaring ember stained my short, more salt-than-pepper hair a clownish orange and etched deep lines in an unfamiliar face. I tried to recall my real face and picked from memories the face in an old Polaroid –a clear-eyed, dark-haired, boy's face, one unmarked by a lifetime of unpaid debts. The black-and-white Polaroid face was as unreal as the ugly, orange face in the mirror. The ugly face was closer to the truth, however.

Who in hell was I anymore? The name on the door read Pete Pinel, Private Investigator – words that had meant something to me once. I said them aloud. The syllables evaporated like sputters of steam from the radiator beneath the window. I hunched over the sink, splashed my face, and listened to water gurgle down the drain. I wiped my face on my shirt sleeve, swallowed the last of the beer, and dropped the bottle in a wastebasket where it clattered against the other dead soldiers. I sat back down and faced the ledger.

So.

I drew my .45 from the shoulder holster. We had a kind of ... not friendship, but certainly a long shared history. A kinship. Perhaps even a next-of-kinship. In the dark the gun looked unfamiliar, like my face had looked in the mirror. But its smell, its weight and balance ... its *feel* was unmistakable. A grip of warm wood. A barrel of cold steel. Heavy, wood-handled steel. Like an ax. Like a scythe. I imagined the sound it would make racking a round, the precise, metallic snicker-snack of machined parts moving with purpose. I hefted it in my hand and judged that it was heavier than the sum of its parts. The excess was a ghost in the machine, a demon that I had summoned many times with IOU's. How heavy that haunted tool must have felt when I pressed it into Ronnie's frail hand her last, hopeless night in the hospital; how hard it must have been to push away.

She chose to wait.

To wait holding my hand instead of the scythe.
That I now held.
In my empty hand.
So.
A bell sounded. Someone had entered the
anteroom. I heard rustling and a gentle rap at
the door. Playing possum, waiting to be left alone
again, I couldn't shake a nagging voice in my
head, and it wasn't Jesus' voice that time.

*Enough already, okay? You win! ... You're the
saddest and most miserable son-of-a-bitch who
ever was. Now will you, please, get your shit in
one bag!*

From a second knock I gathered that it wasn't
opportunity outside. Probably a Goddamm
collector. I holstered the .45 ... ambivalently.

*The bill tolls for thee.*

It wasn't particularly funny, so maybe
something else was funny, because I'm sure I felt
a smile. And for the life of me, I couldn't recall
the last one.

## Chapter Two

When I flung open the door to the waiting room, a white-haired old geezer yelped and stumbled backwards, raising his hands to protect his head. Barefoot, he wore an oversized, buttonless pea coat over pajamas stenciled Camino by the Sea Hospital. The pajamas were a particularly bad sign.

"Tis the wind and nothing more," I said.

"Are you mad?" he croaked.

Talk about projection! Despite a sunken, dead-carp face, the old guy's electric-blue eyes crackled with the kind of energy whose dynamo is secret knowledge of the one true answer to the only big question.

"They were *waiting* for me," he said.

"Lucky for you. Often they leave if you're late."

He peered suspiciously into the dark office. Although he had once been tall and probably beefy, age had left him stoop shouldered and stick-like. The strength with which he suddenly pushed past me to dash to the window was, therefore, surprising.

"They're gone!" he said.

"See what I mean?" I followed him inside, tugged the desk lamp chain and parked facing him. "Who's gone?"

"The men looking for me, you imbecile!"

"Oh, them ... Say, come away from that open window, okay?"

"Three men in black coats." He pointed. "Right down there."

"The ones waiting for the bus?"

"They're gone now!"

"No accounting for that, is there?"

"My God! I imagined you'd have your wits about you."

"C'mon, pal, no offense, but the window has me nervous. Take a seat, okay? ... Got a name?"

"How would they know? I ... I must have said something."

"Loose lips, sink ships. How about that name."

He bounded to the door, cracked it, and peeked into the waiting room. Slamming the door, he flipped the deadbolt.

"I used a payphone. They *couldn't* know, unless ... " He pawed at his pajamas.

"Maybe the transmitter is in your head. Maybe they can read your thoughts."

He froze as if considering the idea.

"Okay, Mr. X, let's get real. You waltz in here barefoot – "

He looked down at his feet, purple from the cold.

"Wearing a coat that doesn't fit over Camino by the Sea pajamas. Camino is the Ritz of ocean-view loony bins. You either ran or wandered away. Trust me. Whatever you *think* is happening has a better explanation."

"Don't condescend you ignorant buffoon! I'm a physician."

"Sorry, Doc, but you're a few pills short of a cure."

He fell silent in an eerie way – just went blank as if the thoughts had been yanked from his head. I waited.

" ... Forgiveness ..." he whispered.

Nothing to say to that, I waited some more. When he looked up, the gleam had returned.

"Do you think it possible?" he said.

"Forgiveness?" I shrugged. "I favor punishment."

"I deserve it, you know?"

"Forgiveness or punishment?"

"Both. For what I found. The philosopher's stone."

Dredging from some college class the medieval notion of a magic catalyst, I said, "So you're an alchemist. You turn lead to gold, do you?"

He placed a green vial from his coat pocket on the desk.

"And back ... to lead ... " he sighed, sinking into a chair.

I unscrewed the vial's black, plastic lid, looked inside, and upended a walnut-sized, rock-candy crystal into my palm. I scratched the crystal with a fingernail and rubbed the finger across my gum. The electric tingle was unmistakable. I dropped the rock back into the vial, replaced the cap, and – waste not, want not – licked my finger clean. My palm, too.

"You found cocaine," I said. "Only they already had it."

"It's … the philosopher's stone." The words seemed to fall from him like weights.

"Sure, sure, lead to gold. Ask Freud or Sherlock Holmes. Been there, pal. I wish it worked."

"Fool!" he snapped, erupting from the chair and throwing his arms toward heaven like Nixon leaving the White House. "Past is prologue."

His jutting wrists were scraped raw and freshly bruised. Camino by the Sea might occasionally use restraints, but they would be soft restraints. Gucci or Prada restraints.

Not handcuffs.

"Who cuffed you?"

"The past we share … *Mr. Pinel.*"

He produced my name as if it were a dove in a magic trick, but since it was lettered on the office door, I held my applause. Nevertheless, if somewhere in time our paths had crossed, a lucid glimmer in his madness might have led him to me. I figured to find out, because the sparks in his eyes were flying. He was fully charged and about to shock me with his one, true answer to the only important question.

He craned forward and placed his lips directly against my ear. "They don't want you to know," he whispered.

"Maybe ignorance is bliss," I said. "Know what?"

"What *actually* happened to Veronica."

It was a breath-stopping moment when gaping pupils froze the world in razor-sharp focus, when the blast of adrenalin that cleared my vision also tensed my eardrums making crystalline every sound. It was as if I were watching myself in some jerky, fast-forward mode – I'm bounding from my chair, I'm collaring the madman, I'm dragging him toward the door. The marks on his wrists were real – not some hysterical stigmata. Whoever had cuffed him might indeed want him back. But if *that name* was the reason, they couldn't have him. The guy was *mine* until he told me what he thought I didn't know.

Almost as one sound, the waiting room bell rang, my office door crashed open and a gunshot shattered the window behind me. Shoving the madman aside, I dove for the desk as feet clamored into the room. Rounding the desk, a giant in a ski-mask saw me ripping the Colt from my shoulder holster and skidded.

"Gun!" he shouted, snap-kicking the automatic from my hand as I raised to fire.

I grabbed his outstretched leg and wrenched him off his feet. Lodging my shoulders in the desk recess, I lurched upward and drove forward like a tank. A gun roared and slugs clanged into the metal desk. Colliding with something softer than a wall, I dumped the desk, spun, and saw a second masked thug holding the whimpering old man while the giant scrabbled to his feet.

"Not in my Goddamm office!"

Charging bull-headed, I strained to grab anything that I could squeeze, crush, or tear apart. Ten years earlier I might have made it, but older, slower, and decidedly dumber, I was dreaming. The giant simply leveled his gun and fired, dead-bang. A hot, yellow blast slammed into my face. Pitched to the floor, I flopped like a beached grunion, my nerves and muscles short-circuiting.

They say the ears are last to go and they're right. As a black rip-tide dragged me away, I heard a screeched, "You can't take what I don't have! I don't know anymore. I don't kn– "

"He's gonna choke on the rag, give'm the needle. And find the Goddamm rock."

"How about that one?"

I felt a kick in my ribs as fade-to-black became oblivion.

"Head shot. He's done."

Philosopher's Stone